He charged me again. This time I met the charge with a quick shove, both my palms square in the center of Alex Smith's chest. I shoved him backward as hard as I could.

Right through the open window.

He lost his balance or something. His arms were flailing, his feet couldn't stop. His butt went through the window, his head shattered the glass at the top. Then he screamed this awful scream. It was a cry of fear, a plea for help, and a scream of agony all in one. Then he just disappeared out the window.

"Oh, my God!" Harris sprinted across the room to the window. "Oh, geez! Look at that. He fell two stories. Look at him! His whole body's all twisted up. Look at his arms and legs! Oh, man!"

I looked over Harris's shoulder. All the guys on the commons had stopped like the players in the world's biggest game of freeze tag. There was no more yelling, no more laughing. Just this big silence.

"He broke his neck," Harris said quietly. "That's why he looks so funny, all twisted up and everything. His neck is broken."

The sound of the crickets and katydids and the crackling bonfire floated in through the shattered window. I didn't realize I had been holding my breath. I let it out with a loud rush.

"You killed him," Harris said. "Before school even started. You killed the most popular guy at Bedford Academy."

FALLOUT

JIM LESTER

LAUREL-LEAF BOOKS

Published by
Bantam Doubleday Dell Books for Young Readers
a division of
Bantam Doubleday Dell Publishing Group, Inc.
1540 Broadway
New York, New York 10036

ISBN: 0-440-22683-X
RL: 5.3
Reprinted by arrangement with Delacorte Press
Printed in the United States of America
June 1997
OPM   10   9   8   7   6   5   4   3   2   1

THIS ONE IS FOR CAMIE,

in appreciation for her love and encouragement.

FALLOUT

CHAPTER 1

A BOY NEEDS A FATHER. At least that's what everyone says. I have four fathers. But it hasn't helped. I'm still a world-champion goofball.

Actually, one of my fathers, my real father, was killed in Vietnam. In a firefight, a surprise attack by the VC. Three days before I was born. So he doesn't really count. I mean, I never even met him or anything. My other three fathers were marine buddies of my real dad's. They all served in the same unit together. My real dad saved the whole platoon before he was killed. He threw himself on a bomb or something.

Then when his three best friends came back home, they sorta adopted me. They came to see my school plays and kid baseball games and that kind of stuff. Gave me super presents like ten-speed bikes and Pac-man on my birthdays and at Christmas. Took me fishing and hunting and to

Cowboys games in Texas Stadium. Stuff like that. Father stuff. So ever since I can remember, I've had four fathers. But, like I said, it hasn't helped. I'm still a screwup.

Being a screwup is what landed me in Bedford. It's a boys' prep school: Bedford Academy, in Bedford, Texas. Forty miles north of Dallas, way out in East Jesus. One hundred years of preparing Texas's finest young men for college and life.

I'm a terminal goofball. Honest. I mean, I don't do dope or drink alcohol (well, maybe an occasional beer). I'm not into shoplifting or stealing cars or anything. (Well, okay, once I did "borrow" our next-door neighbor's BMW. But just once. And I did walk with some junk from the Circle K. Just a couple of times.) But it's mainly little stuff. Like coming home late—or maybe not coming home at all a couple of nights. Or getting a tattoo on my upper arm. The tattoo is really cool—a skull with a lightning bolt through it. I also got an earring without telling my mom. Boy, the tattoo and the earring really fried my mom and my three dads. The earring's gone now. Bedford men don't wear earrings. The tattoo is forever.

Well, okay, so there were a few other things. We did have this big party at Janice Whitehead's house in Dallas while her parents were in New York. Only Janice's stupid parents came back early, while the party was still going on. That was a bad scene. The house was kind of a mess. But we were going to clean it up later, honest. And a couple of the kids were real wasted. I thought Mr. Whitehead was headed for heart attack city.

And okay, I did get caught in bed with Dawn Scott at

2

her house after school one day. Her stupid mother forgot her coat. And my sophomore grades at Thomas Jefferson High School weren't so hot. Straight F city.

To be honest, I didn't like TJ all that much. I got suspended twice for fighting. It wasn't my fault, though. I mean, you can't let anybody push you around. You can't be scared. I played on the soccer team for a while, but I quit. Same with the tennis team. Actually, I have trouble sticking with stuff. I start something and then the next thing I know I don't care about it anymore. I just lose interest. You know what I mean?

Anyway, my mother and all my fathers added my behavior up and it spelled Bedford Academy. Where they make men out of boys.

The Bedford campus was nice enough. Ancient redbrick buildings. Green grass that looked like somebody trimmed the lawn with tweezers. Neatly kept flower beds, geraniums and stuff like that. Cottonwood and sycamore trees. Little benches around the commons. An okay place.

But my first hour at Bedford sucked. I mean, it only took me an hour to screw up. But it wasn't my fault. Honest.

The hour started after I told my mom goodbye in the dorm lobby. All the parents were ushered out, and all the guys shuffled upstairs to their new rooms. Mine was in the middle of the second floor. It looked like all dorm rooms do, like a prison cell. Concrete-block walls. Scuffed and faded tile floor. Thin mattresses on rickety beds. Chipped little desks and chests of drawers that looked like Salvation Army rejects.

It was a couple of days after Labor Day, which in Texas meant it was still summer and still hotter'n hell. Since it was late in the afternoon, the crickets and katydids had started their evening symphony, which I could hear through the open window. I dropped an R.E.M. tape into my jambox and lay down on the stained mattress, crossing my feet over my duffel bag. I had on a pair of jeans and a Dead Milkmen T-shirt, which I had already pitted out because it was so hot. And my black Chicago Bulls cap. Turned around backward.

My new roommate was neatly stacking his socks and underwear and junk in the dresser drawers. He was a dweeb named Mickey Holland. A skinny little guy with stringy dark hair and an Adam's apple that looked like a baseball. He wore this goofy-looking black raincoat. Like he thought it might rain in the dorm or something. Mickey didn't talk much, which suited me fine. We just listened to the music. "Driver eight . . ."

Then all the weirdness started.

Wham! Wham! Wham!

"Oh, God. This is it!" Mickey turned around and looked at me. His face was suddenly pasty white. "The Bedford hazing," he said, "for all the new guys like you and me. My brother went here three years ago. He told me all about it. This is it! Oh, man! Why did my stupid parents make me come here?"

Wham! Wham! Wham!

I could hear guys yelling down the hall. Shoes scraping on the tile floor. Sneakers squeaking. People running.

Mickey sprinted to the window. "There's a giant bonfire on the commons," he said. His voice was shrill, like a girl's. "Upperclassmen are swarming all over the grounds. They're carrying big sticks. I think they're barrel staves. They're gonna paddle us raw!" He turned back around and looked at me. He was trembling. "Aren't you scared?"

"No."

And I wasn't. I really wasn't worried about a bunch of stupid prep-school guys and their moronic little games. I'm not scared of anything or anybody. Honest. You can take that to the bank.

Wham! Wham! Wham!

"They're beating the barrel staves against the walls." Poor Mickey shifted his weight around like he was about to pee his pants. "Oh, Jesus!"

"Monkey and a freshman, sittin' on a rail. Couldn't tell the difference, 'cept the monkey had a tail!" The chant roared up from the commons and echoed through the hall-way.

I sat up on the bed and dug in my duffel bag for a cigarette.

"Let's go, you worthless nerds!" A deep voice came from the hallway just outside our room. "Get out here! There's a fire on campus! Let's go! All of you out in the hall! Now!"

"Monkey and a freshman, sittin' on a rail. Couldn't tell the difference, 'cept the monkey had a tail!"

"Get out here, you little dweebs! On the double!"

Wham! Wham! Wham!

Our door crashed open. "Brace!" The guy was tall and

5

thin. He had on a blue-and-white-striped polo shirt and a pair of wrinkled khakis. He had a barrel stave in his hand.

Mickey froze and hunched his shoulders tight, cupping his fists in front of his chest. I guess his brother had taught him what the prescribed brace was for new Bedford students.

"What's your name, ferret-face?"

"M-M-Mickey H-H-Holland. Sir."

"M-M-Mickey Mouse, if you ask me. God, you're a nerdy-looking little fart."

"Thank you, sir."

"What are you? Junior transfer?"

Mickey nodded.

"Okay, listen, Mouse. Listen carefully. I'm Larry Harris. I'm a senior from Texarkana. I play wide receiver on the best high-school football team in the state of Texas. The Bedford Bulldogs. If you forget any of that, you're in deep dooty. You understand me?"

"Yessir."

"Where are you from, Mouse?"

"San Antonio, sir."

"San Antonio? San Antonio's a town for nerds. Are you a nerd, M-M-Mickey Mouse?"

"Yes—no—sir. I don't know, sir."

"You are a nerd, M-M-Mickey. And don't you forget it!" Harris's spittle flew all over Mickey's face. "Give me twenty push-ups, you little dork. Then you need to help save our campus from the fire. Let's go! Move it, Mouse!"

Mickey dropped to his hands and knees and started the

push-ups. At four his skinny arms began to quiver. At six he collapsed on the floor.

"Whoa! What's your name, big fella?" Harris suddenly noticed me and stepped toward the bed.

"Kenny Francis," I said. "I'm a junior. Transfer from Thomas Jefferson in Dallas."

"Give me twenty, Red. Like your dork buddy. Then we'll get to the fire."

"Don't call me Red." It came out more hostile than I meant for it to. I have red hair and a bunch of freckles and I'm a little self-conscious about it.

Harris looked at me like I had three eyes. "Get on your feet, Red!" He slammed the stave on the top of the desk at the foot of the bed, scattering pens and paper clips and rubber bands onto the floor. "You and the other new students need to put out that fire. Now!"

I took a deep breath and held it. "I'm not gonna do the hazing," I said. "I'm too old. I know it's a big tradition here and all that. But I'm just not interested. All I want is to be left alone."

Harris looked confused. He licked his lips and stared at me. "You . . . you don't have any choice. All new students, freshmen and transfers, all of you go through hazing. It's a Bedford tradition. You got to do it."

"No, I don't."

Harris gnawed on his lower lip. "I said get up and give me twenty! Let's go!" He slammed the barrel stave against the mattress, missing my arm by an inch or so.

"I don't need this." I swung my legs over the side of the bed and stood up. I'm six-two and weigh two hundred

7

pounds. I was into power lifting a couple of years ago (as usual, I quit) and still have a pretty solid upper body. I could tell Harris was impressed.

"That's better, Red." His voice lacked some of its earlier fervor. "Now, give me twenty and—"

"Take a hike, Harris. I told you, I'm not interested. It's nothing personal. I just want to be left alone. You can understand that. It's not hard."

Harris backed up to the door. "You're buying a lot of trouble," he said. "I can guarantee you that. Nobody can get away with this. You'll see."

I shrugged.

"Okay. Let's go, Mouse. We've got a fire to put out." Harris looked back at me. "I'll be back. I promise you that."

I just nodded.

Mickey scrambled to his feet. He paused at the doorway and looked back at me with an expression that hovered between terror and awe. Then he followed Harris out into the hallway.

I dug into my bag and found a pack of Winstons. I lit one with a blue Bic lighter and sucked the smoke deep into my lungs. Welcome to Bedford Academy.

I walked to the door and looked out into the hall. By the stairway, Mickey and the other new students were being herded past the water fountain by a group of upperclassmen, who were yelling and paddling the guys on the butt with barrel staves. The terrified newcomers filled their mouths with water, dropped to their hands and knees, and began to crawl down the stairs that led to the outside.

Back in the room I stuffed the cigarette in the corner of my mouth and pulled a bunch of stuff out of my bag. A framed snapshot of my mother; a picture of my fathers—all four of them in marine fatigues standing in front of this Saigon bar, their arms around each other. Pals forever. Uncle Pat. Uncle Larry. Uncle John. And my real dad—Dickie Francis, onetime star running back of the Bedford Academy Bulldogs.

I put the picture on my desk and crossed the room to the window. Outside, the new guys came pouring out of the dorm on their hands and knees, which were bruised and scraped raw by the trip down the stairs. They were greeted by more upperclassmen brandishing barrel staves. The frightened newcomers were directed to spit the water in their mouths on the fire and then ordered to sprint back to the water fountain on the second floor of the dorm and start the process all over again.

The poor unfortunates who had swallowed their water during the crawl down the stairs were ordered to unzip their pants and use their own water to put out the blaze.

I spotted my roommate standing forlornly in front of the fire, his whole body quaking with fear. Mickey held his penis in his hand, too terrified to pee. A pair of upperclassmen stood behind him, yelling and laughing, unsympathetic to Mickey's plea that he was piss-shy. "Please, please." I could imagine him begging, big tears gathering in the corners of his eyes. I sucked more smoke into my lungs and blew it out my nose.

"Who in the hell do you think you are?"

I turned around. A dark-haired guy who was taller than

I was stood in the doorway. He had chiseled features and a stylish do. His skin was olive-colored, and his teeth looked like they had been polished with a pumice stone. He had on a pink polo shirt and a pair of pressed designer khaki shorts, loafers and no socks.

"Who wants to know?" I took another drag on my cigarette.

"I'm Alex Smith," he said. "I'm the head of the Student Orientation Committee. I'm in charge of seeing that you little dweebs get oriented to life at Bedford."

"He's also the president of the senior class and captain of the football team." Harris hovered behind Smith in the hallway.

"No kidding."

Smith stepped into the room like he owned the place. "I want to know what's going on with you."

"Nothing. Like I told your buddy, I'm not doing the hazing."

"Ole Red's stubborn." Harris giggled, much braver now that he had a partner.

"Don't push me, guys." Everything I said came out tougher than I meant for it to.

"Don't play games with me," Smith said. "Every student that goes to Bedford gets hazed. It builds school spirit. It's the law around here."

"Sorry."

"I'm in charge of this year's orientation, and I won't have it goofed up by some smart aleck who thinks he's better than every other new student in this school. Get your butt downstairs and help your classmates put out that fire! That's an order. Move it! Now!''

"Give it a rest, man. I just want to be left alone and—''

"Hey, look at this.'' Harris picked up the framed photograph of my fathers. "Look at this guy here. The one on the end. I swear it looks just like Mr. Donaldson, the head of the social-science department. When he was young. About a hundred pounds ago. What is this?''

"He was a friend of my father's,'' I said. "They served in Vietnam together. He's one reason my mother sent me here. She thought I needed looking after.''

"Your mama was right,'' Smith said. "You need a lot of looking after.''

"Eat me.'' I took a deep breath, stared right into Smith's big blues, and then flicked my cigarette butt toward his chest. The smoldering cigarette hit him right in the little polo player.

Smith leaped backward. "Hey!'' He brushed the sparks off the front of his shirt.

"Come on, Alex,'' Harris said. "This isn't going to work.''

Smith mumbled something under his breath.

Then he slugged me. Right in the side of the face. It snapped my head back and hurt like hell. It hurt so bad, tears welled up in my eyes.

"Nobody messes with Alex Smith!''

I did. I belted him in the gut. Doubled him over. Made him gasp for air.

"Man, y'all cut it out,'' Harris whined.

I guess Smith didn't hear him. The head of the Orientation Committee and captain of the football team charged me. He came in low, wrapping his arms around my waist like he was tackling some fullback heading through the line. Like two spastic dancers, Smith and I waltzed around the tiny dorm room, holding on to each other's shirts and landing ineffective blows.

"Cut it out!" Harris's voice went up a couple of octaves. "This is getting way out of hand."

Smith broke free and tried a roundhouse right. I blocked it with my left arm and hit him in the face. He staggered backward. His cheek flushed a bright red where the blow had landed. He was crying, big tears running down his cheeks. I was about to cry, my own face was hurting that bad.

He charged me again. This time I met the charge with a quick shove, both my palms square in the center of Alex Smith's chest. I shoved him backward as hard as I could.

Right through the open window.

He lost his balance or something. His arms were flailing, his feet couldn't stop. His butt went through the window, his head shattered the glass at the top. Then he screamed this awful scream. It was a cry of fear, a plea for help, and a scream of agony all in one. Then he just disappeared out the window.

"Oh, my God!" Harris sprinted across the room to the window. "Oh, geez! Look at that. He fell two stories. Look at him! His whole body's all twisted up. Look at his arms and legs! Oh, man!"

I looked over Harris's shoulder. All the guys on the

commons had stopped like the players in the world's biggest game of freeze tag. There was no more yelling, no more laughing. Just this big silence.

"He broke his neck," Harris said quietly. "That's why he looks so funny, all twisted up and everything. His neck is broken."

The sound of the crickets and katydids and the crackling bonfire floated in through the shattered window. I didn't realize I had been holding my breath. I let it out with a loud rush.

"You killed him," Harris said. "Before school even started. You killed the most popular guy at Bedford Academy."

CHAPTER 2

"THE LITTLE DOOFUS IS GONNA LIVE." Uncle Pat fought back a smile, then shoveled a mountain of lasagna onto his plate. "Poor Alex suffered a concussion. And a broken leg. But ole Doc Gillespie says he'll pull through. Alex's parents are, to put it mildly, in an uproar. I tell you, Kenny, you're not making my job as acting headmaster any easier."

The two of us were seated in Uncle Pat's dining room in his ancient Victorian house on the edge of the Bedford campus.

"I told you what happened," I said, trying not to sound defensive. "The guy slugged me. The hazing was a big deal to him. He made it real personal. I'm sorry he got hurt, but it really wasn't my fault. Honest."

Uncle Pat bit off the end of a breadstick. "I'm not surprised Alex jumped into the hazing with both feet," he said. "Alex wants to please. He takes his responsibilities seriously. Senior-class president, quarterback, and all that. He likes to be in charge of everything and everybody. He wouldn't know what 'lighten up' meant."

I chewed off the end of my own breadstick. I was surprised and relieved Uncle Pat wasn't sore at me. I had expected him to do the dance of death on my doorstep. But he seemed okay with everything.

"Alex is nothing like your dad, though." Uncle Pat filled his wineglass from the bottle on the table. "As you've heard a million times, Dickie was class president at Bedford our senior year. And a lot better football player than Alex will ever dream of being. But honors and stuff never went to your dad's head. He took it all in stride. Had a good time with it. Just between you and me, Alex is a pain. The football team will be worthless this year without him. But then again, they were gonna be worthless anyway. The Dogs have been just that over the last few years. Not like when your father and I played for the state title." Uncle Pat paused to remember the good ole days while he filled his mouth with steaming lasagna.

Over the years I've watched Uncle Pat grow. Big and wide. And round. He looks like someone stuffed a hose up his ass and inflated him like a giant balloon. Slowly, a little more air each year. He's a study in circles—moon face, triple chin, beer belly, big ass. His sandy hair is thinning and his head is getting shiny. But the man has a heart as big as the rest of him. It's impossible not to like Uncle Pat. He's a definite white hat.

I also love Uncle Pat's house—an enormous, rambling

old place with all these neat turrets and nooks and crannies and odd little rooms. A guy could get lost in the house for hours if he wanted to. Just disappear with his stamps or baseball cards or whatever. Which is what I used to do every summer. My mom says the house is ratty and run-down, but I think it's like an old pair of Nikes. Snug and comfortable. And safe.

Uncle Pat lives in the house by himself. He had a dog once, a collie. And a wife. But she got run over. The dog, not the wife. The wife just left, suddenly, out of the blue. One day Uncle Pat woke up and she was gone. Mom said it about broke Uncle Pat's heart. She said it made him sad for years. I don't remember the wife. She left when I was just a little kid. Uncle Pat doesn't keep any pictures of her around the house. I don't blame him.

Every room in Uncle Pat's house is filled with these high bookshelves crammed full of history books. American Revolution. Civil War. Napoleon. Hitler. Daniel Boone. Julius Caesar. Ming dynasty. Ancient Greece. You name it. I think Uncle Pat has read every history book ever written.

When I was little Uncle Pat and I would watch TV and eat pizza, and when I went to bed he'd be curled up in his favorite faded blue corduroy La-Z-Boy, starting a thick book—a million-page biography of Abraham Lincoln or something. When I'd come downstairs the next morning he'd still be in the chair, finishing the last few pages of the book. History and food, that's what he loves. Past that, I don't think Uncle Pat cares much about anything. Except red wine. And me.

"Your mom's gonna go ballistic if you get expelled from Bedford before classes even start," Uncle Pat said.

"You think that's gonna happen?" I tried to sound like I didn't care, except I did. I ate some more lasagna. Just like everything else Uncle Pat cooks, the lasagna was fantastic. Sometimes I think he's wasting his time teaching history at Bedford. He could have been a great chef. Cooked a bunch of stuff on TV and been rich like Uncle John. But cooking is a hobby with Uncle Pat. History is his passion.

"Hard to tell." Uncle Pat took a generous sip of red wine from a crystal glass. "Mr. Wellington, the headmaster, had emergency surgery a couple of days ago. Bleeding piles or something. That's why I'm acting headmaster. He thinks the hazing is an important Bedford tradition. Personally, I think it's an idiotic relic of the past. A bunch of stupid jokes designed to humiliate young people. Anyway, while Wellington's gone, I'm more or less in charge. But I can't make any final decisions. All I can do is hold the line until the headmaster gets back. After that, I just don't know. I had to beg and plead and let Wellington win a bunch of racquetball matches just to get you into Bedford. He's not going to like what happened to Alex Smith. I can hear him now. 'I told you if we let a young hoodlum into Bedford, it'd give the school a bad name. I don't care what kind of a hero his father was. We're a preparatory school. Not a reform school for thugs.'"

"Do you think I ought to be expelled? I mean, I told you what happened. It really wasn't my fault."

Uncle Pat drained his wineglass and sighed his most

fatherly sigh. "Why didn't you just go along with the hazing, Kenny? You knew it was coming. You knew it was a big deal at Bedford. It always has been. Why didn't you just go along?"

I felt my mouth pulling into a tight line. "I couldn't," I said. "You know me. I'm not scared of anybody. I got this pride thing. Crawling down the stairs, peeing on some fire while everyone watches, just because some jerk like Alex Smith says I have to . . . Nobody tells me what to do. Nobody."

Uncle Pat rolled his eyes. "I know, I know," he said. " 'Fraid of nothing. 'Fraid of nobody. Since you were ten years old. A ball of courage with feet. You're a piece of work, Kenny, a real piece of work." He tried to act tough, but he didn't make it. This big grin kept toying with the corners of his mouth and peeking out of his eyes. As usual, getting chewed out by Uncle Pat was a piece of cake.

"So am I gonna be out of here or what?" I didn't want Uncle Pat to think I cared one way or the other. But I did. I mean, I didn't necessarily like Bedford. It was stupid and stuffy and full of preppy dorks, but I didn't want to get tossed out, either. To be honest, I wanted to finish one thing—just one thing—I started in my life.

Besides, going to Bedford was a big deal to my mom. And she's pretty cool. Real busy and a little nuts, but cool. She kept telling me about how my real dad and Uncle Pat went there. About what a great school it was. About how it would help me tap my potential, whatever that means. So I guess I wanted to stick around.

18

"Maybe I haven't used up all my chips with Wellington," Uncle Pat said. "I guess my pride can stand a few more losses on the racquetball court. With some luck I can talk him into giving you another chance. We'll just have to wait and see. I promise I'll do the best I can."

I nodded.

"And please call your mom and tell her what's going on," Uncle Pat said.

"Yeah, I will. But you know how busy she's been lately, and—"

"Just call. Okay?" It was Uncle Pat's no-nonsense voice.

"Gotcha," I said. "Right after dinner."

Uncle Pat refilled his wineglass. "Incidentally," he said, staring a hole in me, "lose that Jesus and Mary Chain T-shirt you have on. I can guarantee you Mr. Wellington won't go for that. Bedford's not Andover, but we're still a prep school. You need to look a little more respectable. It won't kill you."

"I gotta be me." I grinned. Uncle Pat just shook his head.

I involuntarily glanced at the portrait gallery in Uncle Pat's hallway, just off the dining room. There was a photo of my real dad in his Bedford football uniform, looking tough and mean, like he could run through a brick wall or something. There was a Bedford team picture with my real dad and Uncle Pat, who played center for the Dogs in those days. There was another picture of the two of them in their football uniforms when they played at SMU, just before they ditched school and went to Vietnam. Uncle Pat says my real dad would have been an all–Southwest Conference halfback if he hadn't gone off to war. There were also a couple of shots of Dickie and Pat in their marine battle fatigues. Friends forever.

"Yeah, but who are you, really?" Uncle Pat said. He sounded serious. "I'm always amazed at the stuff you get into—soccer, and tennis, and stamp collecting, and model airplanes. And weight lifting. And baseball cards. And science fiction novels. It's all here today and gone tomorrow. You're like a bird that doesn't know where to land. What happened to the guitar? John told me he bought you a super guitar."

"He did. A Yamaha. I still play some," I lied.

"What about your studies? Any hope there? I know your grades at TJ weren't so hot. But I also know how smart you are, when you want to be."

I ate more lasagna and chased it with a breadstick. Grades. Stupid, stupid grades. Every parent's great golden idol. The one single thing that makes you an okay human being. If you're making good grades, everything must be all right. Good grades are the mark of a successful, well-adjusted kid. Every parent knows that. Right?

"I don't think school's really my thing," I said.

Uncle Pat leaned back in his chair like your mom always tells you not to, sipped his wine, and looked at me like I was a jigsaw puzzle. Trying to figure out where all the pieces went. I was praying he wouldn't ask me about art. Do you like to draw, son? Lots of parents think that if their kid can't get good grades, maybe he'll be this artistic

20

genius. Ole Kenny's too creative to study math and chemistry and history, but boy, can he draw. He draws all the time. Draws on napkins and old pieces of cardboard. Even toilet paper. Whatever's handy. Not such a brain in school, but he'd put Picasso to shame.

To tell you the truth, I draw like Bart Simpson on drugs. In fifth grade I drew a race car for some stupid project. I put racing stripes and STP ads and all this good stuff on my car. My teacher loved it. She complimented me over and over on what a great-looking cow I had drawn.

Uncle Pat pursed his lips. I knew what was next. You can take it to the bank. Do you like cars, son? Guy is dumb as gum in school, he must like cars. Probably keeps a couple of old T-Birds or 'Vettes up on blocks in his backyard. Takes the engines apart every Saturday. Why, of course he doesn't do well in school. He's going to be a mechanic at the Indianapolis 500. Guy lives to work on cars.

Well, wake the town and tell the people. Kenny Francis doesn't know anything about cars. Forget it. I mean, I know how to start 'em and shift 'em and steer 'em. After that—I'm lost.

Let's face it. Who I am is still a mystery. I'm an okay soccer player. Not World Cup or anything, but okay. And I can pick a few tunes on my guitar. But believe me, I'm no scholar, no artist, and no mechanic. So what am I?

"How about some dessert?" Uncle Pat pushed his chair back from the table. "I made your favorite—a nice coconut cake."

I made a face like I had just smelled a fart. It was a big joke between me and Uncle Pat. Coconut cake. Coconut anything. I hate coconut.

There's a reason for that. When I was a little kid, about nine or ten, I came up to Bedford to visit Uncle Pat. He took me to the movies. *E.T.* Best movie ever. Uncle Pat bought me a Mounds bar. Chocolate and coconut. Yummy-yum. We go into the theater and sit down in the dark and the movie starts and it's wonderful and I'm watching old E.T. try to call home and all that and I tear into the Mounds bar and stuff a chunk of it in my mouth and start chewing and I'm watching the movie and having this great time. Then all of a sudden I realize something is bad wrong. The Mounds bar is alive. I mean, the whole thing is moving by itself inside my mouth.

I sprint out to the lobby and check out the rest of the candy bar. It is alive. Alive with maggots. Zillions and zillions of little white maggots. White strands of coconut come to life, writhing and crawling all over the place. I puked for three straight days. No more coconut. Ever.

"Well, if not a coconut cake," Uncle Pat said, "how 'bout some chocolate chip cookies? I made a double recipe. You can take a tin back to the dorm, share with your roommate. He'll appreciate it."

"Yeah," I said, laughing. "He needs something. Ole Bedford hasn't been too kind to him so far. The hazing scared him to death and the poor guy thinks he drew the original demented roommate from the fiery underbelly of the earth.

"Hi, Mom and Dad." I mimicked a letter home from

Mickey Holland. "Everything is swell at school. I got to crawl down a flight of stairs and pee on a fire, only I couldn't pee and everybody laughed at me. My new roommate just threw the school's quarterback out the window of the dorm and almost killed the guy. I think I'm rooming with an apprentice serial killer. But deep down inside, he's really a good guy. He brought me some chocolate chip cookies."

Uncle Pat laughed.

Before Uncle Pat brought it up again, I went back into the hallway and phoned my mom. For some reason, the connection was bad, the phone lines snapping and crackling. Even through all the static I could tell my mom was really glad to hear from me.

"No, I'm okay, I swear." I had to shout to be heard, and my voice echoed off the walls in the narrow hallway. "Uncle Pat says the guy is gonna be okay. . . . Yeah . . . I didn't mean for it to happen. It was an accident. Just one of those things . . . Nah. I don't think you need to come up to Bedford. I think Uncle Pat can handle everything. . . . Thanks, I appreciate the offer. . . . Right. I'm gonna meet with the headmaster as soon as he gets out of the hospital. . . . Yeah, I will. My best behavior. I promise. . . . No. Really. I think the whole situation is better than it sounds. A lot better, so please don't worry. I'll call you as soon as I hear anything. I promise. . . . Okay, right. Thanks again. I love you too, Mom. Bye."

Along with a father, a guy needs a good mom.

Uncle Pat and I moved out onto the front porch and sat

in the cane-back chairs for a while, just listening to the crickets and watching the lightning bugs as the last of the sunlight faded away. A September evening in Texas. Very peaceful. I ate cookies, and Uncle Pat drank red wine.

"Try not to worry," Uncle Pat said after a while. "I'll do what I can to keep you in school. Alex is gonna be okay. Just go to your classes tomorrow like nothing unusual happened. I'll work on Wellington when he gets back. He's a tough old dog, but I'll do my best to keep you around for a while. No more stunts, though, Kenny. Okay?"

It was a simple question, but I hesitated. I don't like to commit to anything. "Okay," I finally said after a long silence.

"All right. Back to the dorm now. Try to get a good night's sleep. Tomorrow is another day."

Yeah, right. Another day like any other. Only my days never seem to work out like that.

CHAPTER 3

IT WAS INEVITABLE. There was no way around it. Morning had to come.

The day showed up a lot sooner than I wanted. Like about a minute and a half after the sun put in its first appearance. I rolled over, pulled the blanket around my shoulder, snuggled into a ball, and got ready for Son of Deep Sleep.

But I blinked. And when I blinked I saw Mickey Holland sitting cross-legged on his bed across the room, an encyclopedia volume open on his lap. Mickey's hair looked like it had been combed with a Mixmaster. He was wrapped up in his black raincoat.

I shut my eyes tight. I wanted to go back to sleep. Who am I kidding? I wanted to know what my roommate was doing.

"What are you doing?" My voice echoed out of a

25

sleepy fog. I looked at the digital clock next to the bed. It said six and change.

"Hey! What are you doing? It's six A.M.! In the morning!" I threw my pillow across the room. It landed on his encyclopedia. Mickey looked up and grinned. He tossed the pillow back.

"Good morning." He sounded seriously awake.

"What are you doing?"

"I'm reading an encyclopedia article. I read one every morning. They have lots of great information. Like this morning, I'm reading about India and—"

"Are you nuts? It's six A.M. We don't have breakfast until seven-fifteen, classes don't start until eight. What the hell's wrong with you? Tell me you don't do this every morning. Please!"

Mickey sighed. "No." He leaned his head against the wall. Then he started breathing hard, like he was doing some kind of yoga exercise. "No, I don't. To tell you the truth, I'm nervous. Maybe scared. Just a little, you know? I don't like being the new kid at school. Especially after what happened yesterday. I mean, I didn't want to come here in the first place. And things are not off to a good start. This is what I do when I'm nervous. I read my encyclopedia articles. Facts have a calming effect on me."

I rolled over and propped myself up on both elbows. It was too late to go back to sleep.

"It's what I do to calm down." Mickey sounded super-sincere. I almost felt sorry for him.

"I learned to do it back home when my parents got into

big fights. Not the yelling and screaming ones, the serious ones. The throwing-stuff and hitting-each-other ones. All that fighting made me nervous. Even after they split up, they still fight. Like they have to have a dose of combat every so often or they'll die. So I read the encyclopedia." Mickey talked like silence would kill him.

"That's okay," I said. "Whatever turns you on."

"We have algebra together first period," Mickey said. "I looked at your schedule card. Are you any good at math? I'm terrible."

"Same here."

"Why don't we go to the cafeteria together and then go to class?" Mickey begged. "What d'you say? I really don't want to go by myself. Not the first day."

"You're not scared to be seen with me after what happened yesterday? You don't mind walking around with the class psychopath?" I grinned.

Mickey didn't smile at all. "I thought about that," he said. "And the answer is no, I don't mind. Alex Smith is going to be all right. And I hated the hazing, really hated it. I can't believe you just told 'em to back off. I mean, that's really amazing. You probably are a psychopath or something, but you really, actually told 'em to buzz off. I could never do that. You honestly don't care what they think. Whether they like you or not. That's amazing. I always care, I always want them to like me. I just want to be one of the guys. But you know what?"

I had never met anyone who could be that verbal at six A.M. Who could be that verbal anytime. Mickey talked like his tongue had come loose.

"What?" I massaged the sleep out of my eyes with my knuckles.

"It never works. I try too hard. I want the guys to like me too much. I was really unpopular in San Antonio. I mean, the other guys thought I was a total dork. I was always in the running for the Dork of the Decade award. No matter how hard I tried, I always screwed it up."

Mickey never paused for breath. He was like a Niagara Falls of the English language.

"Like this one time," he went on, "we were in stupid PE class. I hated PE. Everybody hates PE. Anyway, mooning was big. Everybody thought mooning was really funny. You know? Wave your bare fanny at somebody. So I'm really trying to be popular, see? Make some friends. So after class I jump up on this bench with no clothes on. And I yell, 'Hey, Fred,' and I moon this guy across the locker room. I really wanted him to like me. But I had to fart. So I thought it would be funny if I cut a big fart, right in the middle of the mooning. So I did. I farted. Only I must have been nervous, because this big turd fell out of my rear. I didn't mean for it to. It just fell out. Right there on the locker room floor. It didn't make me popular, it made me a laughing stock. See what I mean? I always try too hard."

I buried my face in my pillow. I didn't want Mickey to see me laughing. I mean, he was so pitiful, so wound up. I couldn't help but kinda like the guy. He was like a wet dog that showed up at the back door on a stormy night.

"By the way, your tattoo is really sweet. I bet your folks went ballistic when you got it. Right?"

"Right." I looked up from the pillow. "I'll make a deal with you, Mick. If you can be quiet for five minutes while I get out of bed and get a cigarette and get my head on straight, we can go eat breakfast and go to class together. Deal?"

The guy's whole face lit up. "You're on. Not a word. Not a peep. Nothing until you're ready. I swear. Nothing. Not till you give the word. Then we'll go eat together. Then to class. Yeah."

Mickey didn't make the five minutes, but he got close enough. I took a quick shower and put on a pair of black slacks, a white dress shirt, and a tie. A tie, I swear. It's what you have to wear to class at Bedford. A maroon tie. What a stupid thing. It's ninety degrees in Texas in September, and they want you to tie something around your neck and pull it tight. Now that makes a lot of sense, doesn't it?

Anyway, Mickey and I went to the cafeteria in the basement of the dorm, checked in with the counselor, and ate breakfast. The food was okay. Not great, but how bad can you screw up scrambled eggs and toast? Mickey and I sat together at the end of this long table. A couple of the other guys at the table nodded to us. It wasn't exactly friendly, but they weren't giving us the finger, either.

Actually, I was worried about that. I mean, some of Alex Smith's jock friends might just get it in their heads to jump me and get revenge. I wasn't scared or anything, but I was glad nothing happened.

Mickey and I walked across the campus together. We both had our notebooks and stuff in small backpacks. Prep school city. It was five minutes till the eight o'clock bell and the campus was like an anthill. Guys hustling to class, swarming everywhere. Books and notebooks under their arms, backpacks slung over their shoulders. All guys. I never knew how much I liked looking at the girls at TJ.

All the Bedford guys looked alike, except Mickey, who had on his black raincoat. Everybody else looked like something outta *Invasion of the Body Snatchers*. Identical white shirts, black slacks, red ties, short hair. The men of Bedford. Just like it was twenty years ago. Just like it will be twenty years from now.

A lot of these guys were bright. And rich. And had life made. All they had to do was show up. The silver-spoon crowd. All I had was an attitude. An attitude and Mickey Holland. What a combination.

Our first class was in a brick building next to the gym, called Miller Hall. Old Miller probably graduated from Bedford around the turn of the century, made a fortune in oil, and kicked some money back to his old alma mater. Got a classroom building named after him. Oh, wow. The hallmark of achievement.

Miller Hall was terminally geriatric. The tile floors in the corridor were worn from generations of guys shuffling in and out. Our classroom was small and smelled like every classroom I'd ever been in from the first grade on— a combination of chalk dust and floor polish and sweat and fear. Little plastic desks—orange seats with fake wood desktops—sat in rows facing the teacher's desk. Mickey and I slid into the back row. The eight o'clock bell rang.

The room got quiet and a couple of guys giggled. Then everybody settled down.

And nothing happened. I mean nothing.

The room was full. Every seat was taken. Twenty guys just sitting there, staring at the front of the room. A couple of guys coughed nervously. I drummed my Bic pen on the desktop. Mickey squirmed around in his seat like he had to pee.

Then he blew into the room like he was riding the tail of a hurricane. Lots of drama, lots of motion, lots of bluster. He was young, as teachers go. Late twenties. Maybe early thirties. He had on a pressed blue blazer, a blue oxford cloth shirt, conservative red tie, khaki slacks, and loafers with no socks. He was so tan his skin looked like a basketball. His hair was so blond it had to come out of a bottle. I hated him from the word *go*.

"Good morning, gentlemen. And I use that term loosely." His voice was high-pitched and sounded like he had spent some time in England. Or maybe watched a lot of *Masterpiece Theatre*. "I'm Mr. Abernathy. Mr. Richard Abernathy, and this is Algebra II, for those of you who might be lost, and I know there are many of you."

The guy's presence filled up the room. Nobody moved, nobody breathed.

"Welcome back to the outer reaches of preparatory school." Abernathy paced in front of his desk, clasping his hands behind him, talking in a rapid staccato, like a human 9mm handgun. "Let's face it, gentlemen, a Texas

31

prep school is a contradiction in terms. How can you call a place with no crew and no squash courts a prep school? Well, we shall make the most of a bad situation. Even if it's in a place where football really matters. Speaking of that, I understand we have a celebrity in our class this morning. Mr. Francis. Are you here? Please stand up. I'd like to see what you look like.''

I didn't move.

Mickey's eyes were wide. His upper lip was covered with sweat.

I really hated Richard Abernathy.

''Mr. Francis? Please.''

I raised my hand.

''Stand up, please.''

My rear was nailed to the chair. No teacher could scare me. I don't scare.

''I wouldn't think shyness was a problem with you,'' Abernathy said. ''Suit yourself. But understand we'll have no apelike behavior in my classroom. I won't tolerate it. This is my domain, and I am the king.''

My middle finger started itching to take a shot at Abernathy. I resisted the urge. What a jerk!

The next few minutes blurred by. It was Abernathy blabbering about when he was at Choate, this ritzy prep school somewhere back East. Abernathy blabbering about when he was at Harvard. Abernathy talking about his summer in Spain. Abernathy talking about Bach. Abernathy hooting at alternative bands and rap and MTV and the state of Texas.

Then he started talking about math. How math was essential for everyday living. How it held the universe together. How it was tied to logic. Give me a break.

"Let me illustrate with a little puzzle," Abernathy said. "Mr. Francis, please help me out with this." He picked up a piece of chalk from the metal tray beneath the blackboard. He tossed the chalk toward the back of the room. He threw like a girl.

I caught the chalk with one hand. The next thing I knew, I was standing at the front of the room. I mean, it was math class, I had to cooperate.

Abernathy put the puzzle on the board. Three rows of stupid dots.

$$\bullet \quad \bullet \quad \bullet$$

$$\bullet \quad \bullet \quad \bullet$$

$$\bullet \quad \bullet \quad \bullet$$

"The object," he said, "is to connect all the dots. The only rules are you must do it with four straight lines and not lift the chalk off the board. Got it?"

I nodded. I wished Abernathy wouldn't talk to me like I was retarded.

"You can begin anytime."

I nodded again.

I couldn't do it. No way, José. I tried every possible way. I started on the left. Started on the right. Started in the middle. There was just no way. Not with only four lines.

"Take your time, Mr. Francis. Christmas break isn't for a few months."

A couple of guys in the front row giggled.

I was really getting frustrated. Embarrassed and frustrated. I wanted to run out of the stupid room and keep running.

But I stayed. Even though I just couldn't figure the thing out. Not with four lines. Not without lifting the chalk.

"That's enough, Mr. Francis. We'll all be ready for the rest home by the time the answer dawns on you. Go back to your seat."

More giggles. I felt like a stupid piece of garbage. The tops of my ears were burning so much they felt like they were on fire. I pitched the chalk back in the tray and went back to my seat, which suddenly seemed to be located somewhere in Oklahoma.

"Much harder than throwing a fellow student out a window," Abernathy sneered. "But hardly rocket science. Did this ever occur to you?" He turned his back on the class and completed the puzzle with four straight, thick lines.

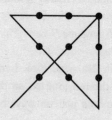

Everybody laughed. Roared. I felt like a total idiot. I hated Richard Abernathy, really loathed him. The jerk never said you had to keep the lines inside the box. That was all I could think of. If you got outside the box, it was easy. I felt like I had struck out with the bases loaded in the bottom of the ninth.

When the bell mercifully rang, Mickey and I packed up our stuff and sprinted for the door. On the way out, Abernathy and I exchanged a look of mutual hatred.

Mickey was too wigged out to talk. So was I. We shuffled down the hall together in silence. I stopped at the water fountain and bent over to get a drink. My mouth felt like west Texas in July.

"Hey, man. You didn't deserve that."

I looked up.

This heavy-set guy was standing next to Mickey. But he was talking to me. He spoke quickly, like he had a prepared speech.

"I'm Tommy Dance. Larry Harris told me what happened in the dorm yesterday. All of it. It wasn't your fault, man. I play on the football team, too. Offensive tackle. To tell you the truth, I wish I'd shoved Alex Smith through a window two years ago. He's a moron from the word *go*. Hang in there, man. Bedford's really not a bad place. There are a lot of good guys here. Give us a shot."

"Are all the classes like that?"

Dance grinned. "Nah. Most of the teachers are pretty cool. Abernathy's a notorious exception. Big, smart Harvard guy. Thought he'd wind up at some hotsy-totsy Eastern school. Bedford was the best he could do. So he takes it out on all of us. He's always talking about how we couldn't measure up to the prep school guys in the East. He thinks we're all a bunch of Texas gorillas. Up his. Don't take what happened today personally. The guy's a jerk. Don't let him get to you."

I smiled at Dance. He seemed like an okay guy. "Thanks."

"I got to go to history class," Dance said. "Mr. Donaldson. Now there is one cool teacher. He's the total opposite of Mr. Abernathy. I'll catch you guys later. We'll shoot some pool down in the rec room. See ya." Dance vanished.

Mickey and I left ole Miller Hall and started across the commons to our next class. Mickey's black raincoat billowed behind him like a cape. The sun beat down, creating little water mirages on the sidewalk.

"I don't think I can take a whole term like this," Mickey said. "I need peace and quiet. Everywhere you go, weird stuff happens. If I hang around with you, I'm gonna have a heart attack or something."

I patted him on the shoulder. The guy was a dweeb, but I couldn't help liking him. "Chill out," I said. "Look at it this way. At this rate, you'll have the whole encyclopedia read before Christmas."

Mickey looked like he didn't know whether to laugh or not.

CHAPTER 4

LARRY TYLER WAS AN AT-RISK KID FROM L.A. But that was a long, long time ago. Before he went to Vietnam and found Jesus. Uncle Pat and my real dad met Uncle Larry in the Marine Corps. They all served in the same unit.

Back then, Uncle Larry was into LSD and pot and long hair and tie-dyed T-shirts and Janis Joplin and Jimi Hendrix. Then his rich family in southern California went ballistic because he was wasting his life. They made him join the marines and do his patriotic duty in 'Nam. And he did. That's when he met Uncle Pat and my real dad and Uncle John and Jesus.

After his hitch in the marines, Uncle Larry came to Texas and studied at the Texas Bible Institute. He became a Baptist preacher. Right now he's the pastor of the First Baptist Church over in Denton. He has this great deep voice that sounds like the voice of God. He reads the Bible every day, and he's always visiting the sick, or marrying people, or burying them, or helping them find Jesus like he did.

When I was a little kid, Uncle Larry was a pretty good dad. He used to take me fishing on the rivers in east Texas. We had a lot of fun. Sometimes we'd go out in the boat and drop our lines and just relax. We wouldn't talk or anything. Just sit and look at the bluffs that lined the river and watch the current and think. We didn't really care if we caught any fish or not.

About a week after that jerk Mr. Abernathy became my personal public enemy number one, Uncle Larry showed up in Bedford. He said he was there to meet with a bunch of Baptist laymen, but I knew he'd really come to see me.

Uncle Larry was staying over at Uncle Pat's, and they invited me to dinner. That was great with me. The food in the Bedford Academy cafeteria was starting to look like pukesville.

Uncle Larry answered my knock on the door and threw his arms around me. "Kenny, Kenny. It's good to see you." That's probably what God will say when you die and go to heaven. He'll throw his arms around you and tell you it's good to see you. Uncle Larry hugged me and patted me on the back. "Come on in here. Boy, it's good to see you. It's been too long. Pat's in the kitchen, cooking up his usual simple fare—barbecued beef, slaw, twice-cooked potatoes with cheese, homemade Texas toast, a chocolate pie. The works." We both laughed. Sometimes

Uncle Pat did get carried away with his cooking, much to our benefit.

Uncle Larry is a truly weird-looking guy. All of his hair fell out during the war. Every last strand of it. His head reflects light. I mean, his dome almost glows in the dark, it's so shiny. He's shorter than I am and has this lumpy, doughy body. Like a walking sack of potatoes. It doesn't help that he always wears a charcoal suit with a blue tie. Always. Never a red tie, or a brown suit, or a sport coat. I suspect Uncle Larry sleeps in his charcoal suit and blue tie. He's that kind of guy. He does everything every day the same way at the same time. Gets up at the same time, prays at the same time, eats at the same time, goes to bed at the same time. Uncle Pat says Uncle Larry is a great guy, but he's a slave to routine.

I said hi to Uncle Pat, who stood in the middle of the kitchen surrounded by steaming pans and boiling pots and spilled flour and ticking timers. The smell of cooking meat permeated the whole house.

"You two go take a walk," Uncle Pat said. "I won't have dinner ready for about an hour. If you hang around here, you'll just mess up my concentration. So go work up an appetite. Then come on back and we'll eat till we pop. Okay?"

Uncle Larry laughed. "Let's go," he said to me. "We'll leave Julia Child alone. Great artists can't be bothered with common folks like us. Come on." He slapped me on the back, and we headed out the kitchen door, banging the screen behind us.

The sun was disappearing over the horizon, and there

39

was a hint of autumn in the air. I had on a pair of jeans and my black Reeboks and a plaid overshirt that covered my Jane's Addiction T-shirt. I left my shirt open, the tail flapping in the breeze.

After a while Uncle Larry started puffing, struggling to keep up with me with his short strides. I slowed down. Since it was dinnertime, there weren't many people out. A couple of guys were tossing a football around in front of the dorm, and this dork from my math class was sitting on a bench under a big oak tree reading a book. The campus was really peaceful.

Just like on our fishing trips, Uncle Larry was quiet. He never forces conversation. I really like that about him. With some adults you feel like if you don't talk, you'll hurt their feelings. Like you're thinking about something else and not them. Not with Uncle Larry. Silence isn't a problem with him.

When we got to the football field, Uncle Larry stopped. It was a well-kept little stadium with about twenty rows of aluminium bleachers on either side of the grass field. The goal posts looked like stick-figure sentries in the twilight. The top of the scoreboard announced that we were standing in front of FRANCIS FIELD: THE HOME OF THE BULLDOGS. There was nobody else around.

"Francis Field," Uncle Larry mumbled. "Pat worked his tail off to get the school to name this stadium after your father. A fitting tribute to a Bedford graduate and war hero. Pat says there's never been a better player on that field than Dickie Francis."

I didn't want to tell Uncle Larry this, but nobody ever

called it Francis Field. The guys just said they were going over to the football field. Or the game Friday night is over at the stadium. I don't think any of the students even know the place is called Francis Field. Or care.

Uncle Larry stared at the empty field for a couple of minutes, like he expected my dad to come charging across the fifty-yard line in his old blue-and-white Bedford uniform. After a while Uncle Larry just shook his head, and we walked on.

All of a sudden Uncle Larry was the one with the quick strides. Little churning steps that left me behind. I had to hustle to keep up with him. We circled Francis Field and crossed the street to the residential area beyond the campus. We hiked past blocks and blocks of bantam bungalows. Some brick, some white clapboard, some stucco, lots of siding. Neatly trimmed yards with freshly painted fences. Basketball hoops over garage doors. Lights were going on in the houses. The dim glow of TV sets shone through the windows.

Uncle Larry and I walked and walked, enjoying the crisp air and the twilight and the comfortable silence. We weren't going anywhere special, just walking.

"Pat says you're facing expulsion from school." When Uncle Larry ends his silence, he doesn't mess around. "You want to tell me what happened?"

I did. I told him about the hazing and that weasel Alex Smith and what happened in the dorm. Uncle Larry winced.

"Do you want to stay at Bedford?" he asked when I'd finished.

"Yeah," I said. "I kinda want to stick it out. I don't have a very good track record for finishing stuff. So yeah, I guess I'd like to stay."

"Tell that to the headmaster," Uncle Larry said, "just like you told me. Pat said you have a meeting with Mr. Wellington next week, when he gets out of the hospital. Just tell him what you told me. No tough-guy stance. Okay?"

I nodded. I hated to admit it, but Uncle Larry was right. A lot of the time I deal with people like I'm mad at 'em. I can't help it. It's like I need to protect myself. I'm not really angry with them, it just comes across that way.

We walked on in silence, skirting a big drainage ditch, crossing a vacant lot. I like Uncle Larry. I like walking with him. Unless he mentions potential. He's big on potential. Personally, I hate that word. I mean, you are who you are. Adults always want to talk about what you might be if you tried harder. And did everything right. And never messed up. Then you'd reach your potential. I've missed my potential by a bijillion miles. I really don't want to hear any more about it.

We cleared the vacant lot and circled a new housing division. Neat little houses in a row. Without saying anything, we finished the loop and turned back.

"How 'bout some dinner?" Uncle Larry said. "I'm starved."

Still no potential. Great.

"Yeah. Me too."

Uncle Larry squeezed my shoulder. Just for a second. It felt good.

On the way back to Uncle Pat's we passed through this cool little residential area. The houses must have been built around the turn of the century or something. They had neat little turrets and framed windows.

"Look down the block," Uncle Larry said. "That's the old train depot. Now it's a bunch of little shops. They've done a nice job with it."

We walked up Castle Street to the old depot. Only now it looked brand-new. The whole place is called the End of the Line. Is that cute or what?

They'd glassed in the entrance to the arcade. Inside, the arcade ran the length of the depot. There were businesses on either side—a shoe shop, a bike store, a craft boutique, an espresso coffee bar called Java River, a restaurant called the Dining Car.

Whoever owned the Dining Car was big on clowns. The whole place was decorated with hundreds of stupid clown dolls. Big ones, little ones. Floppy red hair and silly grins. It was pretty dumb.

"I like it when they recycle old buildings," Uncle Larry said. "Keeps the flavor of the past."

I didn't think it was all that cool, but I nodded anyway. I mean, what's past is past. It's never coming again. It's time to make way for new stuff.

"Let's get some chow," Uncle Larry said. "I bet Pat's almost ready."

"Sounds good."

We took one last look around the End of the Line and headed back down Castle Street toward the Bedford campus.

It was a good thing we were hungry, because Uncle Pat's dinner was world-class. Mountains of juicy barbecue. Cheese-covered potatoes. Cole slaw. Texas toast. Chocolate pie with tiny drops of moisture on the meringue. The best part was the fact that the three of us sat around the dining room table stuffing our faces and didn't talk about me. Or my potential. Nobody asked, Will Kenny get expelled for tossing Alex Smith through the window? What will Kenny do if he gets expelled? Why is Kenny such a goofball? None of it. It was a seriously great dinner.

Over the pie, Uncle Pat told this super story about my real dad when they first got to Vietnam. A bunch of soldiers were shooting baskets on this outdoor court next to the barracks, and this big guy from New York City was standing on the sidelines running his mouth off about how great all the playground players in the city were and how he was one of the best and he could take anybody in the outfit one on one. He was about six-three, and nobody had ever seen him play. He was all mouth. So my dad got hot under the collar and challenged the guy. That was the way my dad was—he didn't take any bull from anybody. One on one. Right then, right there. Make it—take it. Fifteen baskets, win by two, for a hundred bucks. Uncle Pat said everyone gathered round and bet on the New York guy. Made my dad even madder.

The problem was, the New York dude was as good as his mouth. He could dunk with one hand, palm the ball. Shoot the feathery J. He was a player. All the GIs were hootin' and hollerin' and laying down more money. New

York played rings around my dad. The way Uncle Pat told the story, my real father was a great athlete, but only a ho-hum basketball player. Football was his game. He fell behind 14–5.

Uncle Pat said the whole thing was humiliating. My dad couldn't do anything. He couldn't get a shot off, couldn't guard the guy. He was just standing there, out of breath, all sweaty and dirty in his olive-drab Marine Corps T-shirt and fatigue pants, watching the dude do what he pleased. My dad was really getting his rear kicked.

Then, Uncle Pat said, my dad got this strange gleam in his eyes. It was the same look he'd gotten when he played football for Bedford and SMU. When the game was close. A look that said Dickie Francis wasn't going to lose. No way. Not today. No matter how good the New York guy was. Uncle Pat said that when he saw that look he put a hundred bucks of his own down on my dad. The soldier who took the bet laughed at him. Said he hated to take Uncle Pat's money.

Uncle Larry jumped in with the rest of the story. I'd heard it before, but it was so great I loved hearing it again.

My dad came storming back. Long-range jump shots. *Swish! Swish!* Drives to the basket. A head fake and a hook in the lane. 14–13. All the soldiers were going nuts. Yelling and screaming and stomping their feet. Then my dad missed a jumper. The New York guy grabbed the rebound and dribbled back out. It was in-your-face time. The guy faked left, spun right, drove down the lane, and soared into the air like he was never coming down. He was gonna end it all with a one-handed killer tomahawk dunk.

The New York guy reached the peak of his jump and jammed the ball downward toward the hoop. Then it happened. Uncle Larry said it was like a giant bird came soaring out of nowhere. A T-shirted olive-drab eagle. My dad sailed above the rim and blocked the shot. Never touched the guy. Just the ball.

The soldiers went crazy. They screamed and clapped and threw their hats in the air. The New York dude knew it was over. My dad recovered the ball, sank three straight jumpers, picked up a pile of money, and walked back to the barracks. Never said a word. That's the way my real dad was.

After dinner, my dads and I adjourned to the living room. We were all stuffed and a little sleepy from the meal, and it was nice to just hang out. We watched TV. Uncle Pat drank wine and Uncle Larry teased him, telling him he needed to cut down on his drinking. The words were funny, but I could tell he wasn't kidding. Uncle Pat said the wine was from God, the drunkard was from the Devil. They both laughed.

After a while I said good night and headed back to the dorm, taking my time walking across the campus. I felt spooky. I needed to study, but why do homework if you're not going to be in school next week? I was sorta hanging in the air. Maybe yes, maybe no. Maybe in, maybe out. Who knew?

Nobody was outside. The lights were on in the dorm, making the place look like a giant Halloween pumpkin. I could see guys sitting at desks by the windows, doing their homework or writing letters home. I could see other guys moving around in their rooms, shooting the breeze with their roommates or listening to the radio or playing air guitar.

Suddenly I felt at home. Outside, alone in the dark, where nobody could see me or get to me or mess with my head. It was weird.

CHAPTER 5

THE WEEKEND WAS LIKE WATCHING ICE MELT.
Real slow. Real boring. Even the hands of the clock in the
dorm hallway seemed to go on strike.

Nobody likes to wait. Nobody wants to stand in line, or
hang around a bus stop, or wait for a phone call. It gets on
your nerves. Let's face it, waiting is the pits. It's life in
slo-mo.

All weekend I felt like I was sitting in a doctor's wait-
ing room, only the doctor never showed. I was waiting for
Headmaster Wellington to make his big decision. Does
Kenny Francis stay at Bedford or get tossed out? Uncle
Pat called me late Friday afternoon and said His Highness,
King Wellington, was back on the throne, but was
swamped with work and wanted to see me in his office on
Monday afternoon. Hence the weekend wait.

Mickey Holland wasn't much help. He spent most of

his time lying around on his bed, picking his zits and reading the stupid encyclopedia. Mickey couldn't get enough of it. I was bored.

I was so bored I did my homework. That's pretty bored. I did all my math problems in a couple of hours. They really weren't that hard if you sat down and concentrated on them. I read a chunk of *Huckleberry Finn* for my English class. I read a chapter in my history textbook. The Puritans. That was really life in slo-mo.

Most of the time I just sat on the bed and strummed chords on my Yamaha. Did some fingerpicking. I slept a lot. After all this activity, I finally reached Saturday afternoon.

Saturday night there was a stupid dance in the stupid gym. A busload of St. Mary's girls came over. Big thrill. I passed. Not in the mood. In forty-eight hours I was probably going to be history at Bedford anyway. Screw the girls from St. Mary's. Hmmm. That did have a ring to it.

Anyway, Mickey, that geek, went to the dance, and I spent Saturday night in front of the tube. I was asleep by the time my roommate got back.

By Sunday afternoon there was a real possibility I might go crazy. The chances were good that time might stop completely and leave me nuts. On the other hand, being crazy might be better than being bored. Anything was better than being bored.

I called my mom in Dallas just to say hi. I got the answering machine. The message was a big ad for Anthony Powers. My mom works for this dude named Anthony Powers. She's had the job for about a year. She loves it. Powers is a guru in the positive-thinking field. Mom runs workshops for businesspeople—positive customer relations, stuff like that. Uncle John has sent all of his employees through Mom's workshops. I suspect that's why Mom has moved up in the company. Uncle John has a lot of employees. That's a lot of business to bring in.

Just before I crossed the line into nutsville, I grabbed the phone and called Uncle Pat. That's what fathers are for. I explained my situation and asked him if I could borrow his car for a couple of hours. He didn't like the idea, but I think he understood about how tough it was to wait for Mr. Wellington's decision, and besides, the Cowboys were coming on later.

Uncle Pat loves to cook up a bunch of nachos and cookies and stuff and spend Sunday afternoon alone on his sofa eating and drinking wine and watching the stupid Dallas Cowboys play football. God! I can't wait to be an adult.

I slipped on a pair of jeans and a red-and-blue rugby shirt and my Nikes, ran across the campus to Uncle Pat's house, promised to have his Accord back by dark, caught in midair the keys he tossed me, wheeled out of the driveway, and headed south for Big D.

What a disaster.

I covered the forty-minute drive in half an hour. I went by Lee Arnold's house. Ole Lee and I have been friends since we were little kids. But his mom said he was gone and she didn't know where he was or when he'd be back. I tried Janey Farrell's house, but her father said she was spending the weekend down in Austin with her older sister. I circled by the North Park Mall and walked around looking for somebody from TJ. Anybody. No luck.

Everybody had vanished. The whole thing made me a little depressed.

To save the trip from being a total failure, I decided to opt for the Good Family Member award and go visit my grandmother, G.G. G.G. stands for Gran-Gran. It's one of those cutesy little names kids attach to their grandparents when they're too little to know any better. The name sticks, and everybody starts using it. All of a sudden some nice old guy whose name is Fred or Bob becomes Boom-Boom or Gumpa or Gum-Gum or something stupid like that. In my case, Joanne Francis, my dad's mother, became Gran-Gran, which got shortened to G.G. Clever little devil, wasn't I?

To visit G.G. meant a trip to the North Dallas Racquet Club. On any given Sunday afternoon you could always find G.G. at the club. Never at home. There were no tennis courts at home. So I headed for the Central Expressway, turned off at Yale Avenue, and drove out to the NDRC.

The NDRC is a state-of-the-art athletic club. It has everything—swimming, weights, racquetball, indoor jogging track, whatever. Most of all it has tennis. A dozen outdoor courts, a dozen indoor ones. G.G. is a tennis freak. She plays in a couple of ladies' doubles leagues, takes lessons every week, goes off to tennis camps in Florida and Arizona a couple of times a year. She wears little tennis-racquet bracelets and serves drinks in little tennis-ball glasses. She talks about John and Ivan and Steffi and Martina like they live next door or something. Tennis is the only thing she seems to enjoy. Especially since Grandpa Max ran off to Mexico with his legal secretary a few years ago.

The girl at the front desk was a state-of-the-art blond wearing a maroon T-shirt with NDRC across her tits. Nice shirt. She knew G.G. and said my grandmother would be on court four for another fifteen minutes. She said she'd page G.G. and have her meet me in the club restaurant. No sweat.

I went into the restaurant and found a table for two in the back. A waitress came over, and I ordered a Coke and gave the girl my grandmother's club number. I knew G.G. wouldn't mind. The waitress brought my drink, and I said thanks and relaxed.

The Cowboys game was on the TV over the bar. They were playing the Indianapolis Colts. These three men at the next table were whining that the Colts should still be in Baltimore. One guy said yeah, yeah, the Baltimore Colts, and it should be the Oakland Raiders. Like in the good old days. Finally the third guy got all worked up and said if the world was as it should be, the Dodgers would still be playing in Brooklyn. What was wrong with the Los Angeles Dodgers?

I sipped my Coke through a straw, making slurping sounds, and waited. The story of my weekend. I tried to relax, but that wasn't an easy thing to do. The NDRC restaurant looked out over three indoor tennis courts. On the far side of the courts, separated by a green curtain and a glass wall, there was a carpeted aerobics area. The courts were full of mixed doubles, and in the aerobics area a dozen women were throwing their arms into the air, marching in place, stretching and bending in a frantic effort to look like Jane Fonda. Or at least not look like Miss Piggy.

On the restaurant level, a bunch of grim-faced middle-aged men circled the indoor running track above the tennis courts and aerobics class. These guys were not having fun. I mean, what a way to spend Sunday afternoon. Running and running around in a circle. They were all puffing and sweating and punishing themselves for not being young anymore. Boy, I can't wait to be an adult.

On the near side of the lower level a herd of guys in their mid-twenties were pumping iron and flexing their incredible muscles and sweating and flirting with blond girls in Spandex outfits that were so bright they would probably glow in the dark.

I felt like I was about to drown in all that activity and energy.

"So how are the Cowboys doing?"

I looked up into G.G.'s big mahogany eyes. "Scoreless in the first," I said, having no idea how the game was going.

"Oh, great," my grandmother said. "You'd think at least the Cowboys could handle the hapless Dolts. God, bring back Roger Staubach. Even Don Meredith." She pulled up the chair opposite me and sat down. "Good to see you," she said by way of greeting. "It's been a while." Then she flagged down the waitress and ordered a double bourbon in a loud voice.

G.G. was pushing sixty and fighting it every step of the way. She'd had a face-lift and a few tucks here and there. Her skin was stretched tight across her face. Not a wrinkle or a bag or a bump. Her brown hair was dyed a shade too dark, but definitely showed no gray. She dieted constantly and was built like a refugee from Bangladesh. The end result of all that effort was that instead of looking sixty, G.G. looked only fifty-eight.

"My backhand is in a definite slump," she said, drying off her damp face with a little tennis towel that said QUIT WORK: PLAY TENNIS. I thought that was really funny, since G.G. had never worked a day in her life as far as I knew. She was wearing bright red tennis warm-ups that matched the color of her lips, and a white terry-cloth headband circled her head.

"So how ya doin', Kenny?" G.G. has this honeysuckle Southern accent. She grew up in a hick town somewhere in Georgia. She hasn't been back there in forty years or so, but her voice still drips pecan trees and magnolias and cotton blossoms.

"Great. Couldn't be better." That's what G.G. always wants to hear. "How 'bout you?"

"Well, honey, I tell you. It's not easy gettin' old. The circulation in my leg is . . . well, you know about that. And my shoulder? My serve is never gonna be the same. But I'm gettin' by. Doin' all right for an old widow lady."

I don't know why G.G. calls herself a widow. Grandpa Max is still alive. He and his legal secretary live together in Mexico City or somewhere like that.

"So how are things at the academy?" She always refers

to Bedford as "the academy." Like stupid Plato taught there or something. "Are you studying hard? Gettin' the grades? I bet you love the place. Right? Your daddy sure loved the academy. I know you do, too."

I took a deep breath. "Not exactly." I decided to go for the gold. "Prep school's been a, uh, difficult adjustment. Sorta. You know?"

She didn't. Not for a minute.

"Oh, I'm sure you're doing fine." She dismissed my difficulties with a wave of her hand. "The academy is a wonderful school. Only boys from the best families in Texas go there. The academy's graduates go on to Harvard and Yale and Stanford and Rice and SMU."

The waitress put a glass of bourbon and water in front of G.G. and replaced my Coke.

"Honey, y'all need to get the lead out on these drinks," G.G. snapped at the waitress. "Thirsty club members shouldn't have to wait this long. You understand what I'm sayin'?"

"Yes, ma'am."

I smiled and mumbled, "Thank you." The waitress smiled back.

G.G. lit a Winston with a gold lighter, blew smoke out her nose like a dragon, and gulped down half the glass of bourbon. I leaned back in my chair and sipped my Coke.

"Of course, honey," G.G. said, "no one expects you to equal your father's record at the academy. But I'm sure you'll learn to love the place as much as he did. Lord, it was heavenly when he was there. Your grandfather and I would drive up on Friday nights and see all the football games. The band would play and the cheerleaders would hop around and wave their little pom-poms and shake their little tushes. And everyone would cheer when your father carried the ball. It was a wonderful, wonderful time.''

''I'm sure it was.''

''Are you going to play on any of the teams at the academy? I'm sure you'd make some team, even as a sub, if you tried.'' There was a hint of skepticism somewhere in G.G.'s voice. Just behind the mint julep.

I shook my head. ''I'm not into sports much,'' I said. ''I think music is more my thing. I still play guitar some.''

G.G. took a sip and a drag. ''Oh, honey. You'll outgrow that. Your daddy had a tin ear. He didn't care a whit about music.''

I suddenly regretted coming to see G.G. I needed something, but I had come to the wrong place and I knew it.

Sometimes my grandmother's okay. But most of the time she hides behind the wall. She was behind the wall that day. Way behind it. You can see the wall go up behind her eyes. Then she just peeks over the wall to see what she wants to see. After that, she carries on a conversation like you're not even there. She talks at you, not to you. G.G. wants the response to every question to be ''Great. Everything is just great.'' Sometimes things are not so great. But it's real hard to explain that to G.G. when she's hiding behind the wall.

''Well, hon, even if you don't play on any of the teams, you'll do fine,'' G.G. said from behind the wall. ''You'll meet some wonderful young men from the very best families in Texas. They'll be important contacts your whole life through. And please make good grades. That's so important. So you can attend a good college. Your father made wonderful grades. Good enough for Stanford, not to mention SMU. Oh, Kenny, I'm sure you'll grow to love the academy. Just like Dickie did.''

"Yeah, Bedford's a pretty neat place," I said.

I had the definite feeling my grandmother wouldn't want to hear about how I tossed Alex Smith through the dorm window and was waiting to hear if I was going to be expelled from good ole Bedford. I'd have to chuck that information over the wall like a hand grenade.

"By the way," G.G. said, signaling the waitress for another drink, "I— Oh, damn!" Her eyes had drifted to the TV screen behind the bar. I turned around. The Dolts had intercepted a pass and run it back for a touchdown. Way to go, Dolts.

"Oh, the Cowboys have got to find another quarterback. That's all there is to it. Where is that stupid waitress?"

I suddenly longed for the dorm back at Bedford. Even the boring parts. Even my homework. I really missed Mickey Holland and his encyclopedia. Honest. I was genuinely glad it was Sunday afternoon. Glad the weekend was staggering to an end. No matter what the next week held in store.

CHAPTER 6

ENTER THE HEADMASTER'S OFFICE. If you dare.

After a whole weekend of waiting and waiting and waiting, finally I was going to be face-to-face with Mr. Wellington, the meanest prep school headmaster in the galaxy. Fresh from his hemorrhoid surgery. With my whole life on the line. Is Kenny gonna stay or go? Sounds like a rock song.

First you have to confront the guardian of the headmaster's inner sanctum—a woman in her fifties behind a big desk. A stern woman who has been in her fifties since the dawn of man. She has been placed on this earth to make errant students feel small and helpless. She is good at her job. Very good.

The woman asks you to wait. Obviously, you have no choice. The woman has dull, graying hair and dead eyes and smelly breath that would wilt a forest of redwoods.

58

The woman says sit. It's not an invitation. There are no smiles in the headmaster's office. The bench is hard. No one gets comfortable in the headmaster's office. So you wait some more. There's a tiny window behind the woman's desk. Outside, the slate-gray sky of the morning has turned black in the afternoon. The clouds are fat and threatening to explode with rain. A flash of lightning startles the woman. She looks up. Her lips curl around her yellowing teeth in a snarl. How dare the lightning interrupt her endless typing. She defiantly flicks on her desk lamp to combat the growing darkness.

The intercom on the woman's desk crackles. The waiting is over. Mr. Wellington will see you now. Your whole future hinges on the next ten minutes of your life.

I shook my head, like I was waking up from a deep sleep. *What's going on here? What are you scared of? Mr. Wellington?* Fat chance. I'm not scared of Wellington. I don't care how mean he is. What can he do? Throw me out of his stupid school? This is no big deal. *Why?* Because I'm not scared of anybody. No kidding. I just had a momentary lapse or something.

I charged into the headmaster's office unafraid.

Carter Wellington, the headmaster of Bedford Academy, filled up the tiny room like a sumo wrestler in a phone booth. He was so big, I had serious doubts there was enough air in the little office for both of us. His neck strained against the confines of his tight white collar, and the knot in his tie was strangling him, turning his acne-pitted face the color of a rotten tomato. His blue blazer was stretched across his frame like it was about to pop every seam. The man's clothes were tailor-made by Omar the Tentmaker.

The top of his green metal desk was clear. A Mohave of metal. No papers, no books, no files. All the pencils sharpened and arranged neatly in a white ceramic holder. Nothing out of place. I was in trouble.

"Sit down, son." Wellington's voice sounded like it was strained through a lifetime of unfiltered cigarettes. I sat.

"What's your problem, boy?" Wellington leaned forward, rested his elbows on the desk, and locked his fingers under his chin. He was sitting on an inflated plastic doughnut, and every time he moved a little air escaped from the cushion. Hemorrhoid surgery. It was hard not to laugh.

"What d'you mean?" I ignored the little cushion farts and looked serious. It took some effort.

"I understand you don't like the hazing at Bedford. What's the story here? You think you're too good or what? Hazing builds character, son. Makes you part of the school. Part of the team. Only a wimp would object. I understand you went nuts over the thing and tossed poor Alex Smith through the dorm window. Does that cover what happened?" Wellington rained on me, pelting me with his words, his breath, his angry energy.

This was not going to be easy. I cleared my throat. "Not exactly," I said. "I told Smith I didn't want any part of the hazing. He was the one that went nuts." I took a deep breath and exhaled. "And I didn't toss him through the window. After he slugged me, I shoved him and he fell through the window. There's a difference. The whole thing was an accident. *That* covers it." I looked the headmaster square in the eye.

"Is that right?" Wellington compressed his lips into a thin line. He was not a happy camper. "Well, it turned out to be a costly accident, son. The school may get sued, and the football team doesn't have a quarterback. I'm talking *real* costly."

"I'm sorry he got hurt. I really am."

Wellington leaned back in his chair and crossed his fingers behind his head. The cushion farted. I looked at my Nikes and bit my lip.

"Smith's gonna be all right," Wellington said. "His broken bones will heal. He's a gutsy kid. But Smith's not my problem right now, son. You are."

Ah, the crux of the matter. What to do with goofball Kenny Francis. The scourge of Bedford Academy.

"Let me tell you something." Wellington's eyes focused on a spot somewhere behind me, somewhere on the closed door or the wall. The cushion relieved itself. "Before I came here five years ago," Wellington said, "I was the winningest coach in the history of Texas four-A football. I won state titles at Humboldt and at Rock City. My teams were disciplined and hard-working, and they played up to their potential. My motto was 'Be all that you can be and then some.' I've brought that same approach here to Bedford. You understand?"

I didn't but I nodded anyway.

"But now you've come along and put me in a bind." Wellington was angry. "I was brought here to do two things: instill discipline and raise money. And I've done a whale of a job at both. But now you've stumbled in here and made my job tougher than it already is. Way tougher. You understand?''

I looked him square in the eye again. He hated it. He kept looking at the spot on the door.

"Tossin' the star quarterback of the Dogs out the dorm window the first day of school says to outsiders there's no discipline here," Wellington growled. "That tells people Bedford's full of thugs and hoodlums, kids running wild. That kind of bull doesn't happen at Eastern prep schools. Prominent men I contact about Bedford say, 'I don't want to give my money to that place. Bedford's nothing but a reform school for punks.' It's not a real prep school. You see what I'm sayin?''

I nodded. My neck was getting sore from all the nodding.

"Why don't you try saying 'Yessir' every once in a while?'' The man was irritated.

I nodded again.

Wellington didn't like it, but he went on anyway. "My natural inclination is to toss you right out of here. Pure and simple. End of problem. Get rid of the bad apple and save the barrel.'' He let out a long, disgusted sigh.

I kept looking him in the eye. It was a fun game. Wellington couldn't take it. He looked at the door.

"But sometimes things are not that easy.'' The cushion went *pssssss*. Wellington ignored the sound. "Just my luck, you're Dickie Francis's son. That name carries a lot of weight around here. Your father was a war hero in 'Nam. His name's on the big monument in Washington.

He won a chestful of medals. I don't remember your father when he went to school here, though. I had just started coaching over at Sherman. We did play Bedford one night. Pat Donaldson played in the line. I remember him. He was tough. Bedford had this kid named Kinkaid. Best running back I ever saw. He picked up two hundred yards that night. I'll never forget it. Tackling him was like trying to tackle a ghost. The Dogs were something special in those days."

Who was Kinkaid? My father was the best running back in the school's history. Wellington was really a dork. "That's what I hear," I said, trying not to rub the headmaster the wrong way.

"Well, you hear right." *Pssssss.* "Pat Donaldson says he's known you since you were a baby. He was a close friend of your father's. Pat's a great teacher. A credit to the profession. He could have had my job if he'd wanted it, but he's a dedicated classroom teacher. Loves to teach you little punks all about the Civil War and such. Teachers like that are hard to find these days. My other faculty members look up to him. He's been here for God knows how long. I'd like to keep Pat happy if I could. He wants you to stay. Wants me to give you another chance. You understand what I'm sayin'?"

Wellington wanted to expel me real bad, but he couldn't take the heat. He was scared to expel Dickie Francis's son from Bedford. He had a real dilemma. I didn't even bother to nod.

"But if I let you stay here, you'll just mess up again. Believe me, son, I've seen your kind before. A hundred times or more. All of you are alike. Peas from the same pod. If I've seen one of your kind, I've—"

"Hey! Don't do me any favors!" My mouth started operating on its own. As usual. "I'm not scared of you! Your crummy school stinks anyway."

The cushion sounded like a punctured balloon. Wellington leaned forward and smiled.

Stupid, Kenny! He's provoking you. He wants to pick a fight. He wants you to smart-mouth him until he doesn't have any choice but to toss you out. For God's sake, if you want to stay at Bedford, shut up!

Wellington's eyes flashed. It was goodbye Kenny, but something was holding him back. Like an invisible hand on his shoulder. I could tell from the look on his face I'd gone way too far. But for some reason I was still safe. It was weird.

"I have to keep you here at least for a while," Wellington said, writhing under the invisible hand. "But I'm gonna tell you this, you little wisenheimer. All I've got to do is give you a chance. Just a chance. That's all. If you mess up even a little, all bets are off. You understand what I'm saying? I'll be after you with both barrels blazing. And believe me, it'll be my pleasure. From now on, you make yourself invisible on this campus. You're the Invisible Man. You got it? 'Cause if you don't, I'll rain on your parade like you can't believe. As of this moment, you're on official probation and you got one chance. You better take it and make the most of it. You're mighty lucky to be a Bedford student after what you've put me through. You understand?''

I shrugged. I guess it was better than a nod.

Wellington didn't expel me. I couldn't believe it. After I talked back to him and insulted his school. Something was going on, something I didn't know about. Wellington was scared to throw me out.

"That's all, Mr. Francis." Wellington dismissed me with a wave of his hand.

I didn't have to be asked twice. I got up and hustled out of the headmaster's office, sprinting past the gray-haired guardian. My heart was thumping, and I had pitted out my shirt. Carter Wellington was the biggest dork I ever met in my whole life. Bigger than Mr. Abernathy.

Outside the rain had started. Big-time. Giant drops hit the sidewalk in front of the administration building with a plopping sound. I didn't have an umbrella and I didn't feel like running back to the dorm. So I got wet. I ignored the rain and walked across the campus like it was a sunny spring afternoon.

I got soaked, but I didn't care. It started raining harder as darkness dropped over the campus. I just kept walking. Bright flashes of lightning illuminated the buildings and the trees in the commons. Everything was soaked and glistening with the wet. The wind whipped the rain into my face. I kept on walking, like everything was perfectly normal.

But something weird was going on. I could tell. Mr. Wellington really wanted to toss me out of Bedford. But he couldn't do it. Why? Because of Uncle Pat? I doubted it. Teachers don't have that much clout. Because my real dad was a football star at Bedford back in the Stone Age?

Nah. I couldn't really buy that. There was some other reason Wellington hadn't given me my walking papers. I mean, the guy had wanted to kill me right there in his office. I'd given him every reason to tell me to take a hike. I'd all but told the headmaster where to get off. Adults don't go for that.

Besides, if he got rid of me, then he could appease Alex Smith's parents and all the old grads who wouldn't donate to a school full of punks. Goodbye Kenny, goodbye problems. Wellington didn't need a pain like me around. Especially since I shot my big mouth off at him. Why would a tough old coach like Wellington put up with that? Something weird was definitely going on.

Lightning popped, and I jumped. The rain really attacked me. My Nikes were filled with water, making a sloshing sound as I walked across the campus. I slowed down. The storm didn't bother me. It couldn't scare me. I wasn't scared of anything.

Except myself.

If I was honest, really honest, I liked Bedford. I mean, there was a lot wrong with the school. For sure. But it wasn't such a bad place overall. Mickey Holland was a dweeb and all that, but he wasn't such a bad guy. Not really. Sharing a room with him was kinda fun. Even with his goofy encyclopedia. And Tommy Dance seemed like a cool dude.

The schoolwork at Bedford wasn't fun, but it wasn't that hard, either. Bedford was an okay place. So why had I pushed Wellington to toss me out? I'd really challenged the guy to get rid of me. It was like I wanted to get the boot. I guess that's what a goofball does. He sabotages himself. He makes sure he can't get the stuff he really wants. Figure that one out.

Now I had one more chance. But another screwup and Wellington would kill me—before he expelled me.

The rain fell harder, blowing in my face, lashing the buildings and the trees. Lightning snapped and crackled and exploded somewhere beyond the Bedford campus. It felt like the end of the world.

CHAPTER 7

"LOOK OUT THE WINDOW, MAN! It's a tornado! I swear! Check it out!'' I burst into the dorm room, out of breath, dripping water all over the tile floor.

Mickey was sprawled on his bunk, deep in his encyclopedia. "Geez," he said, looking over the top of his glasses. "You look like a drowned dog. Haven't you ever heard of an umbrella? Or a raincoat? Or are you one of those people I'm always hearing about that doesn't have enough sense to come in out of the rain?" He still had on his white dress shirt and tie from school. He also had on his black raincoat. Mickey was strange that way.

"You'll make a great mom someday," I said. "I didn't wear my rubbers, either, Mom."

Mickey giggled.

I peeled off my dress shirt, grabbed a towel from the back of my closet door, and started drying off. The towel didn't seem to help. I felt like the rain had seeped through my skin and soaked my internal organs. The water dripped off me and made little puddles at my feet. There was plenty more where that came from.

"So what's the verdict?" Mickey asked. "Do I have a single room for the rest of the term or what?" He sat up, pushing aside a half-dozen encyclopedia volumes.

"You're not that lucky." I struggled out of my wet slacks and stood in the middle of the room in my boxer shorts, still toweling off like mad. "I turned on all my charm, and His Majesty, King Wellington, said Bedford Academy just couldn't live without me." I slipped on a black Grateful Dead sweatshirt and a pair of jeans. "As long as I don't sneeze or cough or use more than my quota of toilet paper, I can stay here as long as I want."

"No kidding. That's great." Mickey sounded genuinely glad. "I thought Wellington would ax you for sure. He's supposed to be the meanest man in north Texas. I hear he eats live chipmunks. Bites off their little heads. How in the world . . . ?"

"Who knows? Actually, it was kinda strange. To tell you the truth, I really made him mad, talked back to him and everything, but he wouldn't— Oh, never mind. I'll tell you about it later. Hey! No kidding—look out the window. I swear we're about to have a tornado."

Mickey looked back at the open book in his lap. "Not hardly," he said. "Tornadoes can occur any time of the year, but are more likely to happen in the spring or summer. It's a little late in the year now for a twister. Besides, you really need a hot, sticky day. And hail. Hail almost always precedes a tornado. And tit clouds. You need those.''

"What?" I scrubbed my hair with the towel.

"Tit clouds. Honest. One cloud formation that almost always warns you that a tornado's coming is the mammatoform—clouds shaped like women's breasts, bulging downward, by the hundreds. It's in the encyclopedia. I swear. I haven't seen any tits today, so the storm can't be a tornado.''

"If we can't have a tornado until you see tits, I guess we're all safe at least till the turn of the century."

Mickey stuck his book in front of his face. His middle finger appeared over the top. "Big stud," he laughed. "You may see a lot of bazooms, but you're not gonna see a tornado. Not today. I guarantee it."

"Okay, Mr. Knows Everything There Is to Know. Maybe we've got a cyclone out there. Cyclones hit Texas. I know that."

The book came down again. "Geez! Educating you is going to be a major challenge. What you know you could put on a file card. You need to read something besides *Hustler* and *Spider-Man*. For your information, the word *cyclone* refers to any low-pressure area with winds spiraling around and into it."

"Well, aren't we the fountain of all knowledge." I grinned and started combing my hair in front of the mirror on the back of the door. I really did like Mickey. Even if he was a dweeb.

"Well, just so you won't embarrass yourself again, the term *tornado* is a much more specific name for a storm. It comes from the Spanish word for 'turning.' A real tornado represents nature in her angriest mood."

"Old Mother Nature with PMS."

Mickey laughed. "In the worst way," he said. "In fact, a tornado is the most violent storm on earth. I read the whole encyclopedia section on tornadoes this summer. We're actually in the center of what's called Tornado Alley. It's a region between the Rocky Mountains and the Appalachians. It's where cool air masses from the north meet warm air masses from the south. That's how tornadoes get started. When the cold, dry air from the mountains hits the warm, moist air from the south, you get a whirlwind accompanied by thick black clouds and thunderstorms. Then the warm air rises with a spiraling motion, and when it cools it forms a twisting, funnel-shaped cloud. Then—"

"Enough!" I said. "Give me some good stuff. What's the worst tornado that ever hit? I bet you know that." I stuck an R.E.M. tape in the jambox on the dresser. Too much quiet makes me nervous.

Mickey looked like a human happy face. The guy was like a puppy—if you gave him some attention, he went crazy. "The tri-state tornado of 1925," he said. "It started in Missouri and then traveled to Illinois and Indiana—killed six hundred eighty-nine people, did over sixteen million dollars' worth of damage, covered two hundred nineteen miles in less than four hours. It was the

most murderous and destructive twister ever to hit anywhere in the whole world. How 'bout that?''

"You're unbelievable, man. You *are* the fountain of all
knowledge.''

Mickey took a mock bow from his seat on the bed.

Hanging out with Mickey was kinda fun. "Okay, whiz
kid,'' I said. "You know so much, let me ask you a question. I'm gonna stump you. You ready?''

"Shoot.'' Mickey was really enjoying himself.

"The teams at Tulsa and Miami are the Hurricanes.
Right?''

"Everybody knows that.''

"And there's the Iowa State Cyclones? Right?''

"Yeah, right,'' he said. "You must be a closet football
fan.''

"Yeah, sure. Now try this. Name me one college team
that's called the Tornadoes. If a tornado is the worst storm
of all, how come there are no teams called the Tornadoes?
Answer me that.''

"Man.'' Mickey scrunched up his nose, lost in thought.
"There must be one. Somewhere. Let me think. I used to
really be into football. Hummmm . . . There's not one.
Wow. You're right, I can't think of one. Not anywhere.
That's amazing.''

I flopped down on my bed and lit a cigarette. Outside
the rain continued its assault on the dorm, on the campus,
on the world.

"Let me ask *you* a question,'' Mickey said. "If you
think about the answer, you can probably figure it out.''

"Give me a shot." I blew smoke through my nose, but it tickled and I choked and started coughing and gasping. It was not real cool.

Mickey didn't care. Cool was not high on his list. He waited until my fit subsided. "Here goes," he said. "If we ever did have a tornado around here, what would be the worst building to run into for safety? The worst possible place to hide."

What a stupid question. A building is a building. "You got me," I said.

"A church."

"A church? You're kidding."

"No, seriously. When tornadoes hit, churches always get smashed. Honest. I read it in the encyclopedia. Churches always sustain the worst damage."

The guy was amazing.

"If a church is the worst place to be," Mickey went on with a giggle, "what would the safest building be? Think about it for a minute."

It was like Mr. Abernathy's stupid puzzle. I shook my head. I had no idea.

"A saloon," Mickey said with a dramatic flourish. "Tornadoes almost always smash churches and pass over saloons. That's the honest-to-God truth. You always want to run past the church and head for the nearest bar if you want to escape a tornado."

"Get outta here."

"It's the truth. You can look it up." Mickey lit his own cigarette with a little blue lighter. He's a funny smoker.

He never inhales. Just pulls the smoke into his mouth and blows it out. And waves the cigarette around like he's been smoking all his life. It's really a hoot.

"That's weird," I said. "Tornadoes smash churches and skip over bars."

"Sure it's weird. But there's a reason for it. Think about it for a second."

"God likes bars better than churches?"

Mickey laughed. "Not likely. No, really. There's a scientific explanation for it. Think about what a tornado does for a second. How it works."

Too much science gives me a headache. "I give up. Tell me."

Mickey looked like a cat who had swallowed the proverbial canary. "I'm gonna let you work on this one for a while," he said. "You can figure it out if you try."

"Ah, come on, man. You really got me curious. Tell me the answer."

"Later. I promise." He snuffed out his half-smoked cigarette in the little ashtray on his desk. It's a souvenir of a vacation he took with his parents a few years ago. The ashtray is a ceramic state of Florida. It looks like something left over from biology class.

"Oh, by the way," Mickey said. "I meant to tell you when you came in—your uncle John called from Dallas while you were in Wellington's office. What a crazy guy. We must have talked for twenty minutes."

"Yeah. Uncle John's a good guy. A little off the wall

sometimes, but a good guy. He and my dad fought in 'Nam together. In the marines.''

"I hear your dad was a BMOC at Bedford. A long time ago."

I smiled. "That's what I hear. Football. Campus politics. He must have been a neat guy. I never met him."

Mickey looked puzzled.

"He got killed in Vietnam. Just before I was born."

"Wow." It was a whisper. "Killed in Vietnam. Geez."

"So, what'd Uncle John want?"

"Oh, yeah." Mickey looked relieved. "He wants you to come to Dallas to celebrate at his restaurant Friday night. You bozo. You didn't tell me the guy owns Cajun John's. That's the hottest nightspot in Big D. One of the hottest spots in the whole country. It was written up in *Time* magazine. He even invited me to come along. Me. At Cajun's John's. Can you believe it?"

I felt the blood drain from my face. I chewed on my lip. Something was wrong.

A puzzled look crossed Mickey's face at the same time.

"Celebrate what?" I snapped.

Mickey's eyes looked like a pair of CDs. "That's what just occurred to me," he said. "You were still in the headmaster's office, and your uncle John said he wanted you and me to come celebrate puttin' one over on ole Wellington. Or something like that. He didn't exactly say. . . ."

I suddenly lost interest in why tornadoes destroy churches and not saloons. I had a bigger mystery on my hands. Like how Uncle John knew what had happened between me and Wellington. Before it happened. How did Uncle John know we'd have something to celebrate Friday night? How *could* he know? I had this powerful feeling I wasn't gonna like the answer. Not one little bit.

CHAPTER 8

A BOMB HAD GONE OFF IN MY MOM'S NEW CONDO IN DALLAS. At least it looked that way. There was junk everywhere—jeans on the doorknobs, cardboard boxes spilling over in every corner, paperback books fanned out all over the chairs. Little piles of socks, little piles of this, little piles of that. You name it, it was scattered all over the place. The Condo of Chaos.

I didn't mind. That's the way our house always looked before Mom moved to the condo. Neatness is not a friend of my mother's. Not yet, anyway. So I didn't mind the state of the new place. It was just like the old place. Actually, Mom had only lived in the condo for a couple of months. So she really hadn't had time to straighten the place up. No sweat. She'll get cleaned up about the time somebody plants a colony on Mars.

One thing I did love about the new condo was my room.

It was exactly like my room in the old house. Every little detail was just the same: same bed, same blue bedspread, same R.E.M. posters, same oak bookcase, same paperbacks—in the same order. The room felt like home. It might be in a new building, but it was still home. I really liked that. No matter what happened, no matter how bad things got, I could always go back to my room. Having a place like that is not a small thing.

Mom was glad to see me. When she answered my knock, she squealed and hugged me like we hadn't seen each other for a long time. It felt pretty good.

"Oh, Kenny, I'm so glad you're here. I've really missed you."

When we lived in the old house over on Sherman Street I was a major pain in the butt to my mom. A real goof-up. But she always loves me and is always glad to see me.

"I'm glad to see you, too," I said. "Uncle Pat loaned me his car and got me a special pass for the evening. I thought you'd like to hear about my meeting with Mr. Wellington up at school. I wanted to tell you in person. It's kinda good news. I think."

"Wonderful! Come on in. I was just trying to get some boxes and stuff unpacked. I never dreamed moving could be so much trouble. If you live in the same house for fifteen years, it's amazing how much stuff you accumulate. But I'll get it all fixed up eventually. You know me."

I smiled. Yeah, I know Mom.

Her name is Jennifer Francis. Once upon a time she was really beautiful. Like back when she was a Chi Omega at

SMU and was married to Dickie Francis, the star player on the Mustangs football team.

She isn't so beautiful anymore. Now she has a couple of wrinkles that look like the beginning of the Grand Canyon on her face. And she's added a few pounds here and there. But she still has long blond hair and a pretty smile. And she is my mom.

"Come on in and have a seat," Mom said. "Tell me all about your meeting. I can't wait. I'll get you a Coke or something. Come on, come on. I'm on pins and needles."

Mom and I locked arms and marched over the debris into the living room, sidestepping boxes and piles of clothes and books and junk. Mom had on a pair of black slacks and her faded blue SMU T-shirt. She's had the shirt since she and my dad were married. Honest. She wears it all the time, and the shirt is so faded it's really more of a gray color than the original blue.

The shirt says it all about my mom. She's always loved the past. After my dad died, she didn't even date for ten years or so, and even now it's only occasionally. She told me she'd never find anyone like my dad. It was very romantic. But that's the way my mom is. There'd never be anybody quite like Dickie Francis.

I moved some books off the sofa in the living room and sat down while Mom disappeared into the kitchen. The stereo in the corner was playing Marvin Gaye's "Heard It Through the Grapevine." *Big Chill* music. My mother loves that stuff. She has every popular song ever made between 1965 and 1975. After that, zip. Nada. Nothing.

One of the reasons Mom doesn't look so hot these days is the fact that she's worn out from The Search. Ever since my dad died in 'Nam, Mom has been searching for the meaning of life. I mean, looking everywhere. She's tried it all—she's been a Baptist and a Buddhist and a vegetarian and a Republican. She's gone to business college and nursing school and the art institute. She's sold Shaklee and Amway and Tupperware and Mary Kay. She's done the Great Books program and studied with a guru in Boulder, Colorado, and been the Crystal Queen of the New Age. Now she's big into Anthony Powers and the positive-thinking movement. No wonder she looks tired.

"I don't have any Cokes," she called from the kitchen. "How about a club soda?"

"Great." I didn't really expect a Coke.

"Here." She handed me a bottle. "It's not cold. I hope you don't mind."

"No. Warm's good." I took a big sip from the bottle, just to be polite.

"Now tell me everything." Mom sat down in the middle of the floor and looked at me. She doesn't like chairs or sofas. It's a sixties thing. She was drinking Budweiser out of a can.

"So? What happened?"

I exhaled a long breath. "I'm still in." I couldn't help grinning. "At least for a while. The headmaster is gonna let me stay." A long story made short.

"Oh, Kenny, that's the best news ever. I know you didn't mean to hurt that boy. And now you can really make your stand at Bedford. Your father would be so happy. He just loved Bedford.''

''So I've heard.''

''Yeah, I talked to G.G.'' Mom crossed her legs under her and smiled. ''Your grandmother said you stopped by the club. I know she has a way of going on about your dad and his Bedford days.''

''No more than usual.''

Mom laughed. ''Well, he did love it up there. Football and baseball and track and tennis. All the sports. Except basketball. He hated basketball. Thought it was a game for weenies, as he used to say. The truth is, he just never got the hang of it, so he hated it. That was the way he was. If he wasn't good at something, he hated it. And believe me, there were a lot of things your dad hated.''

I was definitely missing something. But that wasn't unusual with my mom. I was sure my real dad had been a better basketball player than she said. I mean, he had to be to take the dude from New York City in 'Nam.

''I'm really pleased, Kenny.'' Mom came out of her reverie. ''Really pleased.''

''Yeah, me too.'' I came out of my own reverie. ''But listen, Mom. I think Uncle John did something to make Mr. Wellington keep me in school. I mean, I sorta smart-mouthed the headmaster, but he's still gonna let me stay. One of the reasons I came by was to ask if you knew anything about it.''

Mom looked puzzled. ''You got me,'' she said. ''I did see John last week, but he didn't say anything. Sorry.''

I exhaled a deep breath and shook my head.

"Tell me all about school," Mom said. "What's it like? How are your teachers? Oh, and what's your roommate like? I bet it's exciting to have a roommate. Tell me all about it."

How do you describe goofy ole Mickey Holland with his black raincoat and encyclopedia? I gave it a shot. I told my mom all about Mickey and my classes and the whole Bedford bit. Mom listened and sipped her beer and smiled and nodded. It was a pretty cool scene.

I was running out of gas and warm club soda when I remembered what Mr. Wellington had said about the Dogs back in my real dad's day. "Hey, Mom," I said. "Did you ever hear of a guy named Kinkaid? Mr. Wellington said he was this big star back when Dad and Uncle Pat played ball at Bedford. It kinda surprised me. I'd never heard his name before. You know who I'm talking about?"

"Kinkaid? You know, that name does sound familiar. I can't place it at the moment. But listen, I tell you what. Out in the hall in the stack of boxes by the door, I think there's one with some old newspaper clippings, and some of your father's football stuff. I was gonna toss it this week. Why don't you rummage through it while I make us some dinner? I've got some fish sticks and Tater Tots in the freezer somewhere. Anyway, go see what you can find."

Mom went back into the kitchen, and I wandered into the hall. I rummaged through the boxes, found the one she was talking about, and started digging. I was excited. I'd never seen any newspaper stories or anything about my real dad. I mean, I knew my mom had them somewhere, but finding stuff in our house was always pretty problematic.

Anyway, I dug through the junk in the top of the box—crinkled recipes for turkey tacos and a million things to do with fondue, hand-drawn maps, flyers for folk music concerts, church bulletins, George McGovern buttons, endless stuff. About three quarters of the way down I found what I was looking for: a stack of yellowed newspaper clippings held together by a little paper clip.

The paper was brittle, and I handled the clippings carefully so they wouldn't crumble. I sat down in the hallway, rested my back against the wall, and started reading.

It was neat stuff. The first clipping was from the *Bedford Daily Journal.* In the corner it said *September 5, 1970.* The headline said SUPER SOPH PACES BULLDOGS TO WIN. Yeah. I knew what was coming. I read on.

Sophomore sensation Bobby Kinkaid paced the Bedford Bulldogs to a 21–7 upset win over the McKinley Tigers in 5-A play last night. Kinkaid, operating out of the left halfback position, rushed for 156 yards in 12 carries, scored two touchdowns on the ground, and returned a punt 68 yards for another TD. To cap off his inaugural night of high-school football, the versatile Kinkaid kicked all three of the Dogs' extra points.

I skimmed the rest of the game summary. *The Dogs line, led by massive center Pat Donaldson, opened some giant holes to launch Kinkaid's runs.* Toward the bottom of the page there was a line underlined in red marker. *Senior right halfback Dickie Francis carried the ball five times for 17 yards.* I looked on the back for more. There wasn't any more.

I thumbed through a couple of other game reports. Pretty much the same. Kinkaid paces the Bulldogs. Kinkaid does it all. The headline on the last article said KINKAID, DONALDSON WIN ALL-STATE HONORS.

> *The District 5-A state champion Bedford Bulldogs placed two players on the Texas High-School Coaches' All-State Team. Sensational sophomore halfback Bobby Kinkaid and center Pat Donaldson made the team. Other Bulldogs also received honors for what was Bedford Academy's finest football season ever. Along with Kinkaid and Donaldson, end Jim Rowe, tackle Donnie Wertz, and quarterback Sterling Jones were named to the all-district team. Guard Steve Elliot and halfback Dickie Francis received honorable mention on the all-district team.*

Honorable mention all-district. That couldn't be right. Not after all the stuff Uncle Pat had told me. I mean, they named the stadium after my father, for God's sake. I didn't know what to think.

"Let's eat!" My mom's voice came from the kitchen. I didn't feel especially hungry, but I put the clippings back in the box and shuffled into the kitchen. Honorable mention all-district. What in the world . . . ?

I couldn't say anything to Mom. The whole thing was so confusing. Honorable mention? I just kept looking at my mother like I'd never really seen her before. She was so glad to see me. She chatted away about Anthony Powers and her friends and the new condo. I didn't even feel much like eating, which was unusual for me. Actually, that was okay. The fish sticks were overcooked. As usual, Mom zapped the Tots in the microwave. No hint of crispness. Just tiny, soggy lumps. Julia Child is safe as long as Mom stalks the universe.

My mom's not a very good cook, but she's world-class at a lot of other stuff. Like listening to all the rotten things that go on in your life. Sometimes you don't need someone to jump in and solve all your problems. You just need them to listen. That's all. Just knowing somebody will listen makes all the difference, and my mom's great at that.

Except that night in the condo, I couldn't talk about the main thing on my mind. I mean, I told Mom about what happened with Alex Smith and my meeting with Mr. Wellington, but I didn't feel right about bringing up the Bobby Kinkaid thing. It just wouldn't come out.

Not that my dad was a taboo subject. Mom and I talked about him all the time, especially when I was a little kid. She's told me all about how they met at this freshman dance at SMU and how they started dating and stuff like that. She's told me what a super dancer he was and how he

85

had this great sense of humor. So it wasn't like we never talked about my dad. But there was something about this Kinkaid guy. So I decided to give it a rest. At least for a while.

Mom and I shot the breeze for a few more minutes. I finally volunteered to help do the dishes, but Mom said she was too tired to worry about it just then. She said she'd do it later. Probably around Thanksgiving. She told me again how happy she was I was going to stay at Bedford. I promised to do better. I've got that line down pat.

We hugged in the hallway, and I went downstairs and hopped in Uncle Pat's Accord. I took the drive back to school slowly. The night was cool, and I rolled down the windows and let the breeze pour over me. The traffic was light, and I kinda went on automatic pilot.

My brain was too full. Alex Smith and Mr. Wellington and Bedford and Mickey Holland and Mr. Abernathy and some guy named Bobby Kinkaid and Uncle John and my real dad and my mom and all the rest of it. A brain can only hold so much.

For some reason, I kept thinking about this time Uncle Larry took me camping in east Texas. We pitched a tent and fished all afternoon and built a big fire and cooked the fish and told stories and had a great time. I woke up late in the night and had to pee, so I left the tent and walked a few feet away and did my business and turned around to go back.

Only I couldn't find the tent. It was so dark. I mean, dark as in the complete absence of light. The moon and stars were hiding behind these thick clouds, so there I was, stumbling around, waving my hand in front of me, hoping I'd hit the tent or something. I must have looked pretty silly. I knew the tent was there somewhere. I just couldn't find it. So I kept stumbling and waving and hoping and groping.

Suddenly I had the same feeling. I mean, I knew the tent was there. I just couldn't find it. It was too dark. So I just kept flailing around. Waving my hand back and forth, trying to locate the stupid tent. Just groping in the dark.

CHAPTER 9

MICKEY HOLLAND HAD GONE TO HEAVEN.

My roommate's eyes looked like a pair of harvest moons, wide and bright. He was afraid to blink. Scared he might miss something. It was all so wonderful. The bright colors, the sharply dressed people, the noise, the music, the girls, the rich smell of spicy seafood. Mickey the dweeb had never been anywhere, except maybe Taco Bell. Now all of his senses were under siege. Welcome to Cajun John's.

I had seen it all before. It isn't that great. Not really.

Mickey and I had ridden the bus in from Bedford and taken a quick cab ride over to Uncle John's place on Melrose Avenue, which is the hot spot in Big D. For the hip, the cool, the with-it people in the with-it city. Mickey and I were as dressed up as we got. I had on black slacks and a funky blue shirt with billowy sleeves. Mickey had on khakis and a pink dress shirt. A couple of wild and crazy guys.

The place was packed. Friday night is fun night. Every table was filled. Guys were slipping the maitre d' a twenty just to get their names on the waiting list. A line outside snaked around the parking lot.

"How long before we can get a table for four?"

"At least two hours," the guy with the clipboard said.

"That's not too bad. We'll wait." Another twenty changed hands.

The maitre d' recognized me. He's a good guy. He waved and smiled and did a little mock bow as Mickey and I waltzed past the line. We circled the crowd in the lobby. Red lipstick, white teeth, dark tans, fancy dress shirts, big muscles, expensive haircuts. Dallas at night. We made our way straight on back to Uncle John's special table, where we sat watching all the action. Uncle John sat across from us.

"This is the third-highest-grossing bar in America." Uncle John leaned forward and raised his voice so we could hear him over the strains of rock music coming from the bar area. A band called Celebrity Toast and Jam was going full-tilt boogy. CT&J was the hottest local band in the Dallas area.

"My Atlanta place is tenth. Denver is fourteenth. That's in the whole country. Each place looks just like this one. A little touch of the Louisiana home country." Uncle John laughed. It was more of a high-pitched giggle.

The inside of Cajun John's is some interior designer's idea of down home on the bayou. Actually, I don't think the designer knew the difference between a bayou and a beaver dam. He had covered the walls with lots of fake knotty pine, hung fishnets all over the place, and put up lots of pictures of cypress stumps and alligators.

"The seafood just about breaks even," Uncle John said. "The bar is where you make the money. That's why I book good bands into all my places. All eight of them. Nationwide. The bands play the whole Cajun John's circuit. Kenny helps me pick out the bands. He knows what people like in the way of rock and roll." He winked at me. It wasn't true, but it sounded good.

Uncle John laughed some more. He's a real happy guy. "You get that solid backbeat goin'." Giggle, giggle. "The toes are a-tappin', the hands are a-clappin', ain't nobody nappin', everybody's havin' fun down at Cajun John's. Everybody's wearing mink, everybody wants to drink." Uncle John was on a roll. "Everybody wants a brew, everybody wants to— Well, never mind. Yeah. They want the beer, the wine, the scotch, the bourbon, the rum. You name it, they want it, I got it. Welcome to the bayou country. Welcome to Cajun John's."

Uncle John's grin stretched from New Orleans to Monroe and back again. He's sorta tacky, but he's a hard guy not to like. He's like Dallas. A little too rich, a little too glitzy, a little too macho. But at the same time impossible to walk away from.

Uncle John is about the same age as Uncle Pat and Uncle Larry. Years ago they all fought the Viet Cong side by side. Age, however, has taken more of a toll on Uncle John than on my other two dads. Age or fast living.

His hair is completely white and he keeps it cropped real close to his scalp. He has a neatly trimmed white beard. Every hair clipped and in place. Uncle John is a short, skinny guy with a Coppertone tan and a gold stud in his left ear. It matches his gold necklace. He always has deep wrinkles and dark bags under his hollow eyes, like he hasn't slept in a week.

The funny thing was, Uncle John really is a Cajun. John Broudeaux from Homa, Louisiana. Part French, part Indian. He has this funny little Cajun accent. When he drinks too much, he talks too fast and his accent gets so thick you can barely understand him. That happens a lot.

"Hey! I got some crayfish comin' for starters," Uncle John said, straightening the paisley handkerchief in the pocket of his white blazer.

Uncle John was right out of *GQ*. His jacket, his blue shirt, his cream slacks, everything looked like it had been pressed five minutes ago. "My special recipe. Real Cajun cookin'. Not like for the tourists. Hey! You boys want somethin' to drink?"

"Sure," I said. "How about a Coke?"

"Yeah, me too. Coke would be great." Mickey's eyes were riveted on this blond waitress across the room. Like all the waitresses, she had on this little pirate outfit that showed off her figure.

"Hey! This is a celebration," Uncle John said. "How you boys like a little splash of Jack Daniel's in them Cokes? Huh? How's that sound? Just a little. What d'ya say?"

Mickey looked at me.

I shrugged. "Why not?"

"Yeah, great. Me too."

An evening with Uncle John is like running a marathon —you don't have much time to catch your breath, and you're exhausted when it's over. He radiates nervous energy in all directions. He talks in bursts, like from an automatic rifle, and he talks constantly. As if silence were a crime. Fun is the name of Uncle John's game.

When I was younger, Uncle John used to take me on all these great trips. The Indianapolis 500, the World Series. We even went to the Super Bowl in New Orleans one year. Fifty-yard-line seats. Last year he gave me two front seats to the Rolling Stones concert in the Cotton Bowl. Everything is first-class for Uncle John.

"You interested in cars, Mickey?" Uncle John asked. "Sports cars, stuff like that?"

"Yeah, I like cars," my roommate said. "My dad had an RX-7. Before he and my mom split up. He loved it. But he had to sell it."

"A good car, to be sure," Uncle John said. "For my money right now, though, the best thing going is the Nissan 300ZX. Great machine. That and the BMW 325 convertible. Super cars, both of them. I got one of each. I can't ever decide which one to drive."

"Life's full of tough decisions," I said, trying not to sound sarcastic.

Uncle John laughed. "It's a toy store, guys. Life's just one giant toy store. You gotta grab the toys you like and start playing. That's all there is to it. Just grab 'em and start playing." He laughed some more. Philosophy is not Uncle John's strong suit.

It's probably his background. He grew up really poor down in Louisiana. He has eight brothers and sisters, and they lived in some kind of Cajun ghetto. In a tar-paper shack with a dirt floor. His father trapped muskrats for a living. Honest. Uncle John never even finished high school. He quit school and pumped gas. Then he joined the marines. That's where he met Uncle Pat and Uncle Larry and my real dad. After Vietnam, Uncle John moved to Dallas and opened a restaurant. He started out cooking Cajun food from recipes his mother sent him. He was a good cook. One thing led to another.

"Your daddy would have gone crazy over the Z," Uncle John said to me. "He liked sports cars. He had a 'Vette when he was out at SMU. He was real proud of that car. He talked about it a lot over in 'Nam." He looked across the table at Mickey. "Kenny's dad and I served together in the war. We were buddies. You could always count on Dickie. He was a man's man."

Now what on earth did that mean?

Mickey nodded solemnly. He didn't know what to say. Who would?

The waitress arrived with the drinks. There wasn't much Jack Daniel's in the Coke. Just a splash, like Uncle John promised. The crayfish was beyond belief. Fat and juicy. Cooked with butter and herbs and spices, and served with this great sauce. I could have made a whole meal on the crayfish.

"This is my party, so you let me order the dinner." Uncle John saluted with his drink. "We gonna get real down home on the bayou."

"Sure." Mickey and I both laughed. Uncle John was having a great time. So were we.

He called the waitress back over. "Hey, my little Nance, you tell Stan in the kitchen this for me, you un'stand?" The waitress nodded. "We gonna have the Creole. The way I taught him, huh? With the good shrimps. The fat ones. You un'stand? And the salad with the works. Huh? Then we get some dessert later. And another round of drinks. These are my boys here. You look after them, you hear? Whatever they want."

The waitress smiled at us. It was a smile that could launch a thousand ships. We were in good hands.

"So here's to your school." Uncle John raised his glass. "To ole Bedford Academy. To their good sense in keepin' you there, Kenny. It's gonna be good for both of you. It's a place where you can find yourself. Your daddy told me all about the place. He loved it. 'I'm a Bedford Bulldog, born and bred, and when I die I'll be a Bulldog dead.' Yeah. And your Uncle Pat? He wouldn't work noplace else. You gonna do fine. You just got off to a rough start. But now, smooth sailing. Everything gonna work out fine from now on. Huh?"

I took a sip of my drink. I didn't really feel like celebrating. I was glad I got to stay at Bedford. But something didn't feel right. Actually, a lot of stuff didn't feel right. You can only solve one problem at a time, though.

I cleared my throat. "Uncle John, why'd Mr. Wellington keep me in school?'' I asked as calmly as I could. ''After what I did, it doesn't make much sense. Especially after what I said to him. My smart mouth got the best of me. Why didn't he give me the boot?'' I suspected Uncle John knew exactly why. I also had a suspicion I wasn't going to like knowing the reason.

'' 'Cause you a good boy. With lots of potential,'' Uncle John said.

''Don't con me, Uncle John. I'm not exactly a great student, I've got an attitude problem, I won't play ball with their stupid hazing, I pushed the school's star quarterback through the dorm window, and I smart-mouthed the headmaster. Bedford Academy could probably survive without me. What's going on?''

The grin never left Uncle John's face. ''You're a smart boy, Kenny. Marks in school don't tell nothin' about how smart a guy is. You know what I'm sayin'? You always have been smart. Just like your real dad. Don't nobody put nothin' over on either one of you.''

''So what's going on?''

Uncle John let out a long sigh. ''Mickey, do me a favor,'' he said, draining his glass. ''Go take a long leak. Check out the band for a few numbers. When you get back, me and Kenny will have all this family stuff worked out, an' then we'll have another drink or two and the best dinner you ever ate. I promise. Huh?''

''Oh, sure. No problem. I'll be back in a little while.'' Mickey scooted out of the booth like his pants were on fire.

Uncle John sucked an ice cube into his mouth and

slurped on it, watching Mickey disappear into the crowded restaurant. He spit the ice back in his glass and then he leaned forward and spoke to me in a low voice. "So how's Pat? I haven't seen the son of a gun in a couple of months. We used to get together every week. And Larry? I haven't seen him since last summer. God! I miss those guys. They're the best. Maybe this winter we'll get together. Go skiing or fishing in Canada. You gotta keep in touch. Good friends ain't that easy to find, huh? And Jennifer? Bless her. Your dad got the finest woman this side of the bayou. And don't you never forget it. There ain't no more like that one. I guarantee you."

I smiled. "Mom's okay. I had dinner with her this week. Her new place is cool."

Uncle John grinned and nodded. I've always suspected he has a little thing for my mom.

"Uncle Pat's the same," I said. "A little rounder maybe, but he's fine. I saw Uncle Larry last week. He's the same, too. Doing the Lord's work. Right on schedule. He asked about you."

Uncle John nodded.

"So enough of beating around the bush, Uncle John. Level with me. What's going on? How come I didn't get bounced out of the academy?"

"Kenny, Kenny. Ever since you were a little kid, no subtlety. Just the hammer. Right to the point. Okay, you got it. You need a place to find yourself, Kenny. You been wandering around in the wilderness too long. No anchor. No direction. I talked to Pat and Larry. And your mom. We all agree Bedford is the place. You got off to a bad start. Big deal. But it's important that you stick around, give the school a chance. You quit too quick. You gotta learn to deliver. So I wanted to give you another chance. All I did was make sure you got that chance. You un'stand?'' Uncle John lit a cigarette and French-inhaled it. Then he blew smoke rings.

I drained my glass and fought back the angry storm I felt gathering inside me. "So what'd you do? Promise to buy new uniforms for the football team or books for the library? Pick up the tab for Mr. Wellington's hemorrhoid surgery?''

"Yeah. A little of all that. That's how the world works, Kenny. You're old enough to know that. That just the way it is. They need some help at the school, I give 'em some help. My boy gets another chance. Not a bad system, if you think about it.''

"Yeah, only I don't think about it." I drew my lips into a tight line. A part of me wanted to slug Uncle John in the mouth. Part of me wanted to hug him and say thanks. I liked Bedford. Maybe Uncle John was right. Maybe it was a place where I could find myself. Whatever that meant. But to have one of my dads buy my way back into the school felt crummy. As usual, I felt confused.

"Just do your best. That's all we ask." Uncle John reached across the table and patted me on the hand. He really liked being a dad. Tacky as he was, I guess I was lucky to have him.

"This is the greatest place ever." Mickey slid back into the booth. "I mean, I just stuck my head in the bar. Listen to that band. Wow. And this guy pointed out these really good-looking girls at the bar. Four of them. He said they're all Dallas Cowboys cheerleaders. Can you believe that? There they were. Not ten feet away from me. Talk about major babes. What a great place!''

Family time was over.

''Wait till you taste my special Creole.'' Uncle John beamed. ''It's a special night. Huh? We celebrate. New starts. Huh?'' He saluted us, winked at me, drained his glass, and signaled for another drink.

The dinner was everything Uncle John had promised. The Creole was spicy and full of plump, tender shrimp. Even the salad was super. Crisp lettuce and mushrooms and olives and tomatoes and onions and some kind of special honey-mustard dressing. Crispy French bread. For dessert we had Cajun John's specialty—a hot-fudge sundae on a cinnamon tortilla. Mountains of vanilla ice cream, rivers of gooey fudge.

I didn't say much during dinner. I didn't have much to say. I wasn't sure whether I felt happy or sad. I was in nowhereland. I was glad I was still in Bedford, but depressed about what it took to keep me there. I had a feeling it was more than new uniforms for the football team.

Mickey and Uncle John really hit it off. Mickey had read a bunch of encyclopedia stuff about Louisiana, and they shot the breeze about Huey Long and Doug Kershaw and jambalaya and crawfish pie and filé gumbo.

Uncle John talked about some racehorse he owned that ran at Louisiana Downs and told some really funny stories about going to sports car races in New Orleans. He also told us about booking R.E.M. into his Atlanta bar and what a hit they'd been. He asked us if we liked slam dancing. Mickey and I both laughed. I thought it was kinda fun. So did Mickey. Uncle John said he'd like to try it. Uncle John will try anything.

When we finished dessert, Uncle John pushed back his chair, lit a cigarette, and sipped his chicory coffee. "Hey!" he said. "I need to drive you two back up to the school. We all get in trouble if I keep you out too late, huh? You're a couple of good guys. You both got a lot going for you. You gonna do all right in the world. You hit the books, keep your noses clean, you do okay up at Bedford, huh?" He laughed out loud. Uncle John was having a good time. Uncle John is always having a good time. In a sad sorta way. He can make me mad sometimes, but overall I'm glad he's one of my dads.

CHAPTER 10

"UH-OH! I'M OUT OF SMOKES." Uncle John crumpled up the empty pack and dropped the crinkly paper and cellophane into the trash bag under the dashboard of his black BMW convertible. "This won't take but a second. I'll still have you guys back by the curfew. I promise." He hit the accelerator.

"Whatever." I was sleepy, curled up in a ball on the backseat. The splash of bourbon and the big meal and being ticked off and all the noise at Cajun John's had worn me out. I rested my head on the seat and closed my eyes. The smell of fresh leather assaulted my senses. The fragrance of money.

Uncle John had covered the forty-minute drive from Dallas to Bedford in thirty minutes. I was content to flop in the backseat and let Uncle John drive and tell his tales to Mickey. I had heard them all. Most of them were pretty good. Growing up in the bayou. Vietnam. Booking rock bands. Super Bowls and Indy 500s. My eyes burned from cigarette smoke and a lack of sleep. I felt seriously tired.

We sped past the interstate sign that said WELCOME TO BEDFORD, TEXAS: HOME OF THE BEDFORD HIGH SPARTANS, THE BEDFORD ACADEMY BULLDOGS, AND THE ST. MARY'S BLUE ANGELS. Home is where you hang your hat.

Uncle John pulled off the interstate at the exit that connected to Cherry Street, which ran right into the academy campus. Just before he hit Cherry, he whipped into the parking lot of the Circle K on the corner. Uncle John always drives like there's a checkered flag up ahead.

Oil stains dotted the asphalt around the gasoline pumps. Crushed paper cups and crumpled napkins and cigarette butts decorated the empty parking spaces in the front of the store. The neon lights burned my eyes. It felt like it was three A.M.

A blue pickup was parked in front of the store. The truck looked like it was built when JFK was president. It was mud-splattered, and rust was working its way up from the bottom, eating away the body like some horror-movie monster. The bumper had a faded sticker on it that said LOVE JESUS.

There was a motorcycle parked in the handicapped space next to the truck. The cycle was an old Harley-Davidson 750 with cracked seats and chipped paint. It was pockmarked with rust spots. The bike looked like it had circled the globe a million times. Uncle John pulled the BMW into a space across the lot from the Harley.

"Come on in if you want," Uncle John said. "I'll just be a second."

Mickey poured out of the car and held the seat back for me. Ole Mick didn't want to miss anything. Not on the greatest night of his life. I mean, who wants to miss a trip to the Circle K? Not me. I scrambled out of the backseat and marched toward the entrance, rubbing my eyes with the back of my knuckles.

"Your Uncle John is about the coolest dude ever," Mickey said in a low voice as we approached the door. "I know he's not your real dad, but he's really something else. He's not like a grown-up at all. He's just cool."

"Yeah, thanks," I mumbled, not wanting to explain the problems of having Uncle John as a father. "Uncle John's all right. I guess I'm pretty lucky. All my dads are kinda cool. In their own way."

I pushed the door open, and the little bell went off. The lights inside were too bright. Too glary. The food packages too colorful. The floor too sticky. I blinked and rubbed my eyes some more. Mickey came in behind me and wandered over to the cookie section to check out the Oreos. I stopped at the newspaper rack and skimmed the headlines in the *Dallas Morning News*. PLANO WOMAN SLAYS HUSBAND. RECESSION INEVITABLE. MIDDLE EAST UNSTABLE. Headlines that never change.

Uncle John was standing to the side of the checkout counter, waiting for two guys to pay for their stuff. It was gonna take some time. One of the guys was drunk, slurring his words and struggling to stand up. He was a tall man, somewhere in his early thirties. He had a black Willie Nelson T-shirt stretched over his beer belly, to the point that Willie looked liked Dom DeLuise. The guy had on oily jeans and a denim jacket he must have borrowed from his little brother, the sleeves hitting high on his wrists. His dark hair was shoulder-length and greasy, and his unkempt beard was flecked with gray. A faded Red Man baseball cap rested on the back of his head at an odd angle. His BO greeted me at the newspaper rack.

"Ah, come on, man," the guy said to the clerk behind the counter. "You got the beer. I got the money. Forget the State of Texas. Let's do some business." He pronounced it "bi'ness."

The clerk, a smallish guy with blond hair and wire-rimmed glasses, looked nervous. "Gimme a break, man. I can lose my job selling beer after hours. You know that. There's nothing I can do. Y'all go on home now. Ya hear? Mary Alice will be worried about Art." He nodded at the other man.

Red Man's companion, Art, laughed. But it wasn't out of humor. "Yeah, if she ain't out with one a' the Thompson boys again." He was a little wiry guy with leathery skin, a bushy mustache, and a three-day growth of stubble. He had on a plain white T-shirt with holes in the yellowing armpits and a pair of stained khakis. A battalion of bluish tattoos marched up and down both arms. One look at the guy and you knew the lights were on but no one was home. Or ever would be.

"Jest sell us the beer," Red Man said. "Ain't nobody gonna know."

The clerk shook his head. "I can't do it," he said. "The

store's on probation as it is. One more mistake and I'll lose my job. I got kids at home. I just can't do it. It's the law. Sorry.''

"Yeah, you are sorry,'' Art growled. "A sorry so-and-so.''

Mickey moved up beside me. "Rednecks,'' he whispered. "Beer-swilling Bubbas from Raven Glen. I've been hearing about them from some of the guys at school. The word is, don't mess with 'em. They're all meaner'n hell. Most of them are the product of generations of incest. Their mothers and their aunts are the same people. It makes 'em funny in the head.''

"What are you talkin' about over there, boy?'' Red Man weaved away from the counter and faced us. "Wipe that ugly grin off your face.''

"Yes sir.'' Mickey snapped to attention.

"Yes sir?'' Both rednecks cracked up laughing. "Hey, boy. You don't need to salute. Jest shut your mouth.'' More laughing.

"Hey, you little pansies look like you up way past your bedtime. Does your mommas know where yer at?'' Red Man wasn't the only one who was drunk. Art had had his share, too.

"Maybe their mommas know the Thompson boys, too, and don't care where they're at.'' Red Man sniggered. He was a regular stand-up comic. Art didn't think it was funny. It ticked him off.

Uncle John shook his head. "Leave the boys alone, man. I just need to get some cigarettes and we're out of here.'' He laid a five-dollar bill on the counter. ''Gimme a couple of packs of Vantage.''

''Hey, don't cut in line, man. That ain't polite.'' Art whirled around and shoved Uncle John away from the counter.

''Come on, Art. Don't cause no trouble.'' The clerk sounded scared. ''I'll have to call the sheriff's office if you do. I can't have that kind of trouble around here.''

''Let's go, guys.'' Uncle John started toward the door. ''I don't need cigarettes that badly. This is none of our business.''

''What's your problem, you scrawny old geezer? You chicken or what?'' Red Man stepped right in front of Uncle John.

''Excuse me,'' Uncle John said, trying to step around the guy.

''Hey, man!'' Red Man cut Uncle John off, stepping in front of him. ''I'm talking to you! You hear me? I don't like the way you look. I don't like your cute little beard and your cute little earring. You remind me of a cute little pile of dog mess.'' He stuck his jaw out.

Uncle John let out a sigh. ''You've had a little too much to drink. Why don't you go home and sleep it off?'' Uncle John tried to step around him again.

''Why don't you kiss my you-know-what?'' Red Man reached out and grabbed Uncle John's necklace, jerking it forward until it broke.

''Hey, back off, man!'' The voice didn't sound like me even though it came from my mouth.

"Chill out, Kenny." Mickey grabbed my arm. "This isn't the dorm, man. This is really dangerous."

"Let's go, Kenny," Uncle John said. "These jerks are not worth it. Believe me. Just go get in the car and we'll be out of here with no harm done."

"You got a big mouth, kid." Art moved away from the counter and stood next to Red Man. "You got anything to back it up?" He started clenching and unclenching his fist.

"Hey, I'm not scared of you." It was me. Out of control. "You can't just push people around. You don't scare me a bit." The voice that was coming out of my mouth sounded like it was coming from someone else. From far away. Like maybe Mars.

"I reckon somebody needs to teach you a lesson."

"Well, it won't be you, you redneck jerk."

Uncle John put his hand on my chest. "Shut your big mouth and go get in the car. Right now."

"I'm not scared of him." The voice from Mars got louder. "I'm not gonna back down from him. Stupid rednecks! They think everybody's scared of them. Well, I'm not scared at all."

"You better get on out of here," Red Man said. "Art's a little guy, but he ain't nobody to mess with."

Uncle John shoved me toward the door. "Out! This minute."

I didn't budge. I was furious. The rednecks were running us out of the Circle K, like they owned the world or something. I couldn't believe it.

What I really couldn't believe was Uncle John's face.

He was scared of Art and Red Man. I could see it in his eyes. A guy who had fought the Viet Cong. Scared. I couldn't believe it. He pushed me out the door onto the sidewalk.

"Git on out of here, you little wimps!" Art charged. He kicked Uncle John in the leg just as we went through the door. The blow had to hurt because Uncle John let out a little cry of pain. I could hear Red Man laughing inside the Circle K. Laughing at us.

I lunged at the door. Uncle John grabbed me around the waist and we waltzed around the parking lot for a second. "Don't be stupid, Kenny. Get in the car! Now! You're not going back in there!"

I struggled. Uncle John was stronger than he looked. "I'm not scared of him!" I was in orbit. The stupid rednecks had kicked Uncle John. Ripped off his necklace. Insulted him. It was payback time.

"Come on, man. Chill." Mickey's voice was shaking, he was so frightened. "Those guys probably have knives or razors or something. Let's just get out of here and get on back to the dorm."

Mickey opened the door of the car and pulled the seat back. Uncle John steered me into the backseat. "Settle down, Kenny," he snapped. "Believe me, this isn't the time or the place. Just get in the car and shut up." His voice was angry but even. It said "Don't argue" with a lot of authority.

I tumbled into the leather seat. Tears welled up in my eyes. I was so furious I could barely see. I couldn't believe we were backing down. "Why didn't you fight?" I yelled as Uncle John got in behind the steering wheel. "He broke your necklace. He called you names. Why didn't you fight him? We could have killed 'em! Just the two of us! Just you and me!"

Uncle John started the engine. "No, we couldn't," he snapped. "I'm not that tough. And I have serious doubts that you're that tough. Your courage is admirable, son. But it's really misplaced. Dukin' it out with a pair of drunk rednecks in the local Circle K is not a test of anybody's manhood. You put too much emphasis on physical courage, Kenny. You got to have some sense as well. This is life, son, it's not the movies. You got that? Guys like those rednecks are not worth it."

"I'm not scared of any of them!" I couldn't hold still. My body lunged back and forth in the backseat. I started pounding on the leather like it was a punching bag. My lower lip was shaking so hard it was about to jump off my face.

"Kenny, listen to yourself." Uncle John's voice got real calm. "No one has said you were scared. But son, believe me, everyone gets frightened once in a while. It's called being human."

"I'm not scared of anybody!" It sounded stupid and I knew it.

"Every great coach knows when to punt, Kenny. Every great general knows when to retreat." Uncle John threw the BMW into reverse and eased out of the parking space. He turned around and paused. "Ya gotta know when to change tactics." He slammed the accelerator to the floor as he jerked his foot off the brake.

The BMW shot backward like a rocket. The sound of crashing glass and grinding metal echoed over the Circle K lot as the Harley fell down and the car crunched over it. It was like the big pickups going over cars at a tractor pull.

"Oh, man!" Mickey caught himself with his palms on the dashboard. I tumbled onto the floor.

Uncle John grinned, put the car in drive and pulled out of the lot, the tires squealing on the pavement. He started laughing and sped down Cherry Street toward the academy. Suddenly the whole thing was a lark to him. A big joke.

I climbed off the floor and looked at Mickey. My roommate didn't know whether to laugh or cry. I didn't, either. I didn't know what to think. Everything had happened so fast. I was glad Uncle John had crushed the bastard's bike. But I still wished we had crushed his head. Somehow the whole thing just didn't seem right. It seemed a little chicken.

Mickey's eyes were wide and his mouth hung open. Total shock. Uncle John is not your run-of-the-mill father.

"What's that smell?" Uncle John kept his eyes on the road.

"It's me," Mickey said, suddenly sniffling. "I got scared in the store. Those guys were really mean-looking. I thought they were going to kill us. I peed my pants. I couldn't help it." He sniffled again.

Uncle John reached over and patted Mickey on the shoulder. "It's okay, son," he said. "It's called being human. Being human is not the worst thing in the world. Not by a long shot."

CHAPTER 11

WHAT A WEIRD WEEK. Kenny Francis on his best behavior. No fights. No failures. No screwups. Honest.

It wasn't easy. On the outside I played it cool. Inside I was angry. I stayed mad all week long. Like always. I live my life just below the boiling point. I was still mad at Mr. Wellington for putting me under the microscope. Still mad at Uncle John for buying my way back into Bedford. Still mad about the rednecks at the Circle K. Sometimes I have trouble letting stuff like that go. Mad should have been my middle name. It'd be more accurate than Richard.

But mad or not, all week I put my best effort into being a Bedford student. Just like I'd promised I would. Shirt and tie. Sit up straight in class. Finish my algebra problems every night. Memorize my poem for English. Recite it with gusto. Raise my hand and answer questions in Uncle Pat's class. What caused the American Revolution? No sweat. Kenny knows. Answer the questions at the end of chapter five in my blue notebook. Biology? You got it. What are the major species? A neat list in my green notebook. I even went to bed when the dorm counselor called lights out every night. My Bulls cap stayed on the back of the door all week. Pretty nauseating, huh?

To be honest, I didn't study all the time. I shot pool in the dorm lounge with Mickey and Tommy Dance and a senior named Jon from Houston. Jon was okay. Good pool player. I lost five bucks to him. For a good football player, Dance was awful at pool. I won five from him. He was a fun guy. I mean, we weren't tight or anything, but Dance was right. There were some good guys at Bedford.

The week almost got away from me once. Tuesday afternoon, right before supper, Jon and I were shooting pool in the rec room. We weren't playing for money or anything, just shooting around to kill time before the chow line opened. We were the only guys in the place.

The sun was going down, and the shadows from the window stretched out across the green felt of the pool table. A little nine-ball before supper, a nice way to pass the afternoon.

The rec room was located in the dorm basement. The place had a low ceiling and a musty smell. The floor tiles were worn and the furniture had seen better days. The single pool table had also been around the block more than once. The rec room was cozy or cramped, depending on your point of view.

I racked the balls and broke to start the game, but in the middle of my first shot the door from upstairs opened and a couple of guys drifted in. One of them was a burly linebacker on the football team named Andy and the other one was a skinny wide receiver named Chad. Football practice had just ended. Both guys' hair was wet and plastered down from their showers, and their school shirts clung to their damp backs.

I kept on shooting while Andy and Chad draped themselves over the sofa in the corner and started watching.

The door opened again, and Tommy Dance and three other football players came in. One of the players was Larry Harris.

Dance and I exchanged nods and smiles, and he headed for the Coke machine. I sank the three ball in the corner pocket. Harris perched on the stool behind the pool table and started spinning a cue back and forth in his hands.

"You want the next game?" I hadn't spoken to Harris since Alex Smith disappeared through the dorm window.

"Naw, I've had enough games," he said.

I managed a weak smile and bent over the table to size up my next shot.

"We've all had enough games," Chad said sharply.

Suddenly the rec room got real small. I felt my grip tighten on the pool cue.

"Games where we get our butts beat." Chad left the sofa and walked over to the window.

"Like our opener last Friday night." Andy stood up. The guy looked like he had spent half his life in the weight room. Giant arms, no neck. "Gainesville whipped our butts forty-seven to zip. Ran our asses into the ground."

Dance looked at me and shrugged. My guess was the football team had just endured a practice from hell.

"Coach says we're a bunch of pansies," Chad said, turning away from the window. "But you know what? It's not our fault."

Chad was getting on my nerves.

"Yeah, it ain't our fault," Andy said. He and Chad weren't talking to each other. They were just talking. And the more they talked the madder they got.

I had a strong suspicion my week of exemplary behavior was about to come to a screeching halt. I could feel trouble filling up the tiny rec room.

"Naw, it ain't our fault." Chad said.

I missed my shot.

"If we had a decent quarterback, we'd be kicking butt instead of the other way around," Andy said.

"You got that right," Chad added.

Jon lined up his shot, sighting down the cue stick. He was nervously chewing on his lower lip.

"I dunno," Dance said, opening his pop can with a loud whoosh. "It's tough for one player to make that much difference on a football team."

"If that player happened to be Alex Smith, it'd make a humongous difference," Andy snapped.

Dance grimaced.

Jon missed his shot by a mile. Everybody watched the cue ball rebound and roll across the table. Jon backed into the corner.

"Andy's right," Chad said. "If we had Alex, we could

throw the ball more, loosen up the defense. It'd be a whole different season if we had Alex. Right, Red?''

He was talking to me. I bent over and lined up my shot.

"Did you hear me, Red?''

Everyone was staring at me.

"I heard you.'' I focused on the four ball.

"You think you're pretty tough, huh? Big tough guy. Guy that cost us our whole football season.'' Chad said.

I sank the four with authority.

"Yeah, Mr. Tough Guy.'' Andy jumped off the sofa.

I circled the table and lined up my next shot.

"The whole season's down the tubes. Without Alex we can't beat the girls from St. Mary's.'' A boy-mountain of a lineman named Ben moved toward the pool table. The other players called him Gentle Ben. It was meant to be ironic.

I knew what was coming. A bunch of football jocks were about to take their frustrations out on me. No problem. I wasn't scared.

"Alex was the glue that held our team together.'' Gentle Ben was into sports clichés.

"You said it,'' Chad said.

I bent over the cue ball. Chad, Andy, and Ben lined up on the opposite end of the table. They were working themselves into a frenzy. They were doing a good job.

I sank my shot in the side pocket and stood up.

Ben moved to the left of the table and Andy fanned out to the right.

I was surrounded. I looked across the room at Tommy

Dance. He shook his head in disgust. Then he nodded. Just enough to let me know I wasn't alone. It was gonna be brawl city.

"Somebody needs to pay for what happened to Alex," Andy said, clenching his fists.

"Yeah, like the guy who did him in." Chad was bouncing up and down on the balls of his feet like a boxer. All three jocks stared holes through me.

I stepped away from the table and brought the pool cue up to my chest. Samurai pool shark.

"Give it a rest, guys." Larry Harris tapped his pool cue on the floor. He straightened his back and looked at his three buddies. "I miss Alex as much as any of you, but I was there that day and this isn't right. Francis didn't do anything except defend himself."

"What are you saying?" Words were not Gentle Ben's strength.

"I didn't say anything before because I like Alex and I didn't want him to look like a jerk. But I'm telling you now, Alex started it with Francis." Harris's voice was shaking. What he was doing wasn't easy. I was impressed.

"Huh?" Gentle Ben was out of his league.

"Alex got carried away with the hazing," Harris said. "Francis didn't have any choice. He did what any of us would have done. He fought back. It wasn't his fault." Little beads of sweat gathered on his upper lip. He looked miserable.

The three jocks stared at Harris. They had worked themselves up to fighting pitch and now nothing was going to happen. They didn't have a clue what to do next.

Chad shuffled back to the window.

Ben picked the eight ball up off the table and looked at it like it was a moon rock.

Andy looked at me. Everybody got real quiet.

"Sorry, man." Andy's voice was a whisper.

I nodded.

Dance saluted me with his pop can. He had a big grin on his face.

I turned around and looked at Harris. He managed a smile. "Let's go get some chow," he said. "You guys come with us." He indicated Jon and me. "Send the school a message."

It was over. Just like that. I couldn't believe it. Good behavior was still the order of the day. Sometimes you never know.

So all in all it turned out to be an okay week. Kenny on his best behavior, buddies with the jocks. I didn't even see Wellington once. Word was his piles had made a roaring comeback. I hoped so.

On the other hand, it was also a weird week because I couldn't shake this premonition that I was about to blow everything. I live with this constant feeling that any minute I'll make the wrong decision. The bad choice. It's just a matter of time.

Despite what happened in the rec room, I kept waking up at night, sweating, fretting, worrying, not knowing where I was for a minute. Replaying the day before. Was it okay? Did I do something that might come back to haunt me? Did I plant the seeds of a screwup?

By Friday night I was beat. Being a good boy will wear you out. Mickey went to town with Jon and a couple of other guys to see the new Freddy Krueger movie. They invited me, but I passed. I just wanted to be by myself. If I'm alone, I can't screw up.

Indian summer had settled over Bedford during the week, so after Mickey left I opened the window and let the warm breeze soak the room. I slipped on a pair of blue Umbro soccer shorts and and a gray T-shirt and lay down on the bed, listening to the sounds of guys out on the commons, cars in the distance, a stereo from down the hall. Stupid Hammer. Some people will listen to anything. I laced my fingers behind my head and closed my eyes and listened. Indian summer in north Texas.

After a while I wanted to talk to someone. Not about homework or hanging out or how cool it would be to have your own apartment. I wanted to talk about other stuff. Like the stuff in my head. The important stuff.

I wanted to talk real bad. I got up and flipped on the overhead light and looked at the phone. I called my mom, just to shoot the breeze, but all I got was the answering machine. Ditto with Uncle Pat. I tried a couple of my old TJ friends. Not too many people home on Friday night.

I prowled around the room, thumbing through note-books, sharpening pencils, shooting baskets at the trash can with wadded-up paper. I even opened a volume of Mickey's encyclopedia. Kalidasa was the most famous writer of the post-Vedic period of Sanskrit literature. Oh, wow. Big deal. Booooring.

Then this idea got in my head—and it wouldn't go away. A monster idea. The perfect end to the weird week. The idea wouldn't let go. It was so goofy, I loved it. I had to do it. I wanted to do it.

I sat down at Mickey's desk and looked at his Macintosh. I had played around some with a Mac. Games and stuff. The computer was user-friendly. Piece of cake. Turn it on from the back. *Beep.* The screen lit up. Wiggle the arrow with the mouse. Click on the word-processing program. The screen went blank. Okay so far. I typed a *D*. The letter appeared on the screen. I was in business.

If I was gonna make my monster idea come to life, I needed atmosphere. So I got up and turned off the light. Put my Bulls cap on backward. Now you're talking. The computer screen glowed like a giant's eye in the dark room. Great. I found a pair of candles in Mickey's desk drawer. The guy was ready for a power failure. I stuck 'em in Mickey's little glass holders and lit the wicks with my lighter. Flickering flames. More atmosphere. Then I needed music. Can't have atmosphere without music. This was really getting fun.

Digging around in my tape holder, I found what I wanted. I shoved the tape into my jambox and cranked up the volume. The tape was old and scratchy. "Something in the way she moves . . ." The Beatles' *Abbey Road.* "Maxwell's silver hammer went . . ." Great. The sound-track of the sixties. His music, not mine.

Back to the computer. Hunting and pecking by candle-light with the warm Indian summer breeze teasing me, I typed my butt off.

Dear Dad:

I've got all this junk in my head, and you're the only one I can talk to. I'm really sorry you're dead. Boy, am I sorry. I mean, everything would have been so different if you hadn't decided to be such a hero and save your platoon. Man, things would have been different.

Not that everybody's not trying to help. They really are. But you know how it is. Mom loves me, but sometimes she gets tired of me. I just keep screwing up. Sometimes things get away from me. I can't seem to finish anything—you know, see it to the end. I guess I'm kind of a quitter.

I slouched down in the chair and scrolled back over what I had just written. The breeze stopped. It felt like summer had returned. I lit a cigarette with my lighter and sucked the smoke deep in my lungs.

My other dads are doing their best to help me. I swear. They're the best guys in the world, but it's not working. And I sure don't make it any easier. Fights and failures. The story of Kenny Francis. But it's not all my fault. Honest. Like the other night, Uncle John treated my roommate and me to dinner at Cajun John's down in Dallas. But on the way home, these redneck guys started hassling us. I wasn't scared. You and I would have killed the suckers. But Uncle John got scared. Uncle John made us run. He treated me like a little kid. I was really mad.

I stopped for a minute and looked out the window. A big harvest moon hovered over the trees at the edge of the campus. Good night for werewolves. Good night for weird stuff. I puffed on my smoke and thought some more about Art and Red Man. The idiots. My real dad and I would've kicked rears and taken names. No doubt about it.

And Uncle Pat? He doesn't get out of the house much anymore. He just stays inside and eats and reads history books. He's getting fatter and fatter. And balder and balder. He's just an old fat guy who teaches history at Bedford. He is a good teacher, though. I'm in his class. He makes some of that boring stuff pretty interesting sometimes. You can tell he really loves it.

I stretched my arms. What a gas. Writing letters to dead people.

I saw Uncle Larry the other day. He's still doing good deeds. Trying to save everybody. He's still holier than Mother Teresa, running around helping people. Sometimes I just don't get Uncle Larry.

There's a lot of stuff I don't get. The main thing I don't get is me. The best thing about me is that nobody pushes me around. Nobody. But I don't know what makes me tick. It's kinda hard to figure out. I mean, I'm pretty good at sports, but I don't really like them. Not like you did. I'm not stupid or anything, but I don't like school. It's boring. I feel like I'm learning a bunch of stuff that doesn't really matter. Who really cares about algebra and history? Bedford's okay, though. I see why you liked the place. There are some good guys here. My roommate's a good guy. He's sorta goofy, but basically I like him. I hope I finish here. Graduate. Wouldn't that be something? But everyone's waiting for me to screw up, and I probably will.

The tape ended, and I dug another one out of the bin. Enough of the old stuff. *Abbey Road* was my dad's music. I needed a hit of my music. Red Hot Chili Peppers. Yeah. RHCP. Turn up the volume. Back to the keyboard.

I wish I could be more like you. But I'm just not. I know you're disappointed in me. If we met, you probably wouldn't like me. I don't participate in stuff like you did. I just hang out a lot. Everybody says you were a great guy. Nobody says that about me.

Maybe we'll meet someday. Like in heaven or somewhere. Wouldn't that be something? Just walking down the golden streets one day and there you are. "Hey, Dad. How's it going, man? Good to see you."

Yeah, that would really be something. Me and you together. Maybe someday. Well, until that time I guess all I can say is I'm sorry. Sorry for all the bad stuff I've done. I'm really going to try to make it at Bedford. Make you proud of me. I'm going to study hard and not get in fights and not quit. I promise. So, till I see you on the golden streets—

Love,

Writing a letter to a dead person made me sad. It's a sad thing to do. I clicked Save and then Print, and the paper jumped and the printer started shimmying and shaking and rattling and printing.

I lit another cigarette on the candle flame and walked over to the window. The campus was peaceful. The wind blew the leaves across the commons. Everybody had gone to the movies or was taking a weekend in Dallas or somewhere. It was just me and Bedford.

My eyes filled up with tears. Like a baby or a girl or something. How disgusting. Maybe it was the cigarette smoke.

Suddenly Mr. Sad took a hike and I felt real calm. Just like that. Like the calm pills had kicked in. Way down inside I felt like everything was going to be all right. I wasn't going to screw up anymore or fail at anything else or get in any more fights or any more trouble or quit anything.

I usually feel like the roof is about to cave in on my head at any minute. Calm is unnatural for me. It felt super. Do some people feel this way all the time? What if I felt this way all the time? What would I have to do to feel this way all the time?

The printer stopped, and I ripped the letter out. *Good job, Kenny. Radical letter. Truly awesome. Write my dead dad.* Made me feel calm. Monster idea. Monster letter. Now all I had to do was deliver it.

CHAPTER 12

I DIDN'T SLEEP ALL NIGHT. I was too excited. My great idea had expanded, taking on a life of its own. I had to see it to the end. There was no other way.

Mickey came in about eleven, but I pretended to be asleep, lying on my bunk, facing the wall, scrunching my body up into a ball and pulling the blanket tight around my shoulders. My great idea was my secret, and if I couldn't talk about it, I didn't want to talk at all. Mickey suspected I wasn't asleep, so he started blabbering.

"What a sweet movie," he said. "Ole Freddy traps these chicks in the locker room at their school. They're all running around in their underwear, squealing and yelling and trying to cover themselves up. It was great! Then Freddy traps this one major babe in the shower and he's leering at her and waving his metal fingernails around and she turns on the hot water to protect herself, only nothing but blood comes out of the shower head, and then . . ."

I could smell pizza on his breath all the way across the room. I pulled the blanket tighter.

Mickey prattled as he walked around the room, turning on his electric fan, taking off his clothes. Then he turned on his bedside light, jumped into bed, and started reading his encyclopedia.

A couple of hours later, I got up and turned off the light. Mickey was lying on his back, snoring like some old man, the encyclopedia open on his chest. Big-time Friday night.

I got back in bed and closed my eyes, but nothing happened. I just lay there and listened to Mickey make gross noises with his mouth. The stink of pizza farts filled the room. My great idea played over and over in my mind, better and better every time.

I must have dozed or something, because when I rolled over again dim sunlight peeked through the window, making those little cylinders of swirling dust in the air. Saturday dawn. All quiet on the prep school front.

I slipped out of bed and climbed into a pair of jeans, a dirty black Grateful Dead T-shirt, and my black Reeboks. I stuck my Bulls cap on my head. Backward. The way everybody wears 'em. I retrieved my letter from under my pillow, folded the pages, stuck them in the front pocket of my jeans, and headed out. I didn't even bother to brush my teeth.

The dorm counselors were all asleep and the front door

was locked until eight, so I crawled out the window of the men's john on the first floor. Piece of cake.

It was warm and foggy, moving toward another glorious Indian-summer day. I hiked across the campus, feeling like I was the last person left on the planet. I mean, dawn on a Saturday morning in Bedford is dead city. There was nobody around. No people. No cars. Not even any dogs. Just me. Me and the sun creeping over the hills.

I wasn't exactly sure where I was going, but I knew the general direction. On the other side of Cherry Street was this strip of muffler shops and cheap furniture stores and used-car dealers. I knew I had to walk to the end of the strip and turn right. After that, I wasn't real sure.

After I turned, I went down an avenue where these creepy old houses were spread out, fronted by good-sized lawns. Most of the houses were neglected, like old grannies in a rest home. The grass was overgrown, and Coke cans and Lone Star bottles and crumpled cigarette packs decorated the ill-kept yards like ugly wildflowers. All the houses begged for paint.

The leaves still on the trees were turning orange and red, and the dead leaves already on the ground crunched under my Reeboks.

When the houses ran out, I hiked past a row of vacant lots where people had dumped their old bedsprings and sofas and refrigerators. I crossed a railroad track and then there it was! At the end of the block. Just like I remembered it.

A pair of stone pillars supported a sign over the entrance. MOUNTAIN VIEW CEMETERY. What a hoot. There wasn't a mountain within five hundred miles of the place. And who was there to view a mountain, anyway? A bunch of dead people?

I'd only visited Mountain View once. My mom hauled me out there when I was about ten. Uncle Pat went with us. It rained that morning and everything was wet. The grass, the trees, the road. Uncle Pat gave me a couple of Reese's Peanut Butter Cups to take away the gloom. All I really remember about the trip was getting gooey chocolate all over my blue pants and white shirt.

I knew what I was looking for was under this huge oak tree next to the dirt road that wound through the cemetery, so I looked for the tree. Unfortunately, the place was covered with trees.

There was nobody alive in Mountain View, so I figured nobody would care if I just wandered around until I found what I was looking for. I mean, I couldn't hurt anything or mess anything up. So I walked from tree to tree reading the headstones.

Unbelievable. Everybody's life in a couple of lines. JOSEPH R. JOHNSON: BLESSED FATHER, BELOVED HUSBAND. 1913–1968. *Sorry, Joe. You were gone before I got here.* I wondered what Joe was like when he was a kid. Did he get in fights? Goof up? Or was he a do-right guy? Class officer? Jock? Hero? I guess it really didn't matter. Not for old Joe. Not anymore.

JANE WITHERSPOON: 1930–1982. That didn't tell you much. I wondered if Jane had been a looker in school. Did she make good grades or have fun or what? Did she like to read or sew or dance or watch TV? Was she somebody's mom? Wife? Girlfriend? I'd never know.

JACOB ROTH: GOD'S WILL BE DONE. 1971–1975. Oh, man! Jake was just a kid. A couple of years older than I am. Well, not anymore. I guess I passed him by. But geez. Four years old. He missed a lot. A lot of garbage. Maybe old Jake was the lucky one. Dead before he had time to goof up. I didn't want to think about it. I moved on to the next tree.

When I saw the headstone, it took my breath away. It wasn't real fancy. Just a big ugly gray slab. Crossed American flags carved at the top. RICHARD KENNETH FRANCIS: 1953–1973. The end. Nothing about what a great football player he was, or . . . Or was he a great football player? I was starting to have my doubts. Uncle Pat always said he was. But the clipping I read at my mom's condo said Bobby Kinkaid was the big star. My dad was only honorable mention. Not that that was anything to sneeze at, but still . . . The whole thing made me wonder.

I reread the tombstone. Just the facts. Nothing about how my dad was president of the student body at Bedford or played football for SMU or how he saved his platoon in 'Nam. Or how everybody loved him and thought he was such a great guy.

I sat down cross-legged beside the marker. I suddenly felt weak, like I hadn't slept for a long time. Maybe I should've eaten breakfast. I took a deep breath. Now I wasn't sure what to do. Suddenly I felt a little silly. It had seemed like such a great idea in the dorm. When I was alone with the candles and the cigarette smoke and *Abbey*

Road and the glow of the computer screen, it had been a monster idea. Now it didn't seem so hot.

Whatever. I had to give it a shot. I was tired of starting stuff and then quitting. I wanted to see something through to the end. No matter what. I fumbled around in my pocket. The letter had gotten crumpled up.

I unfolded the letter and smoothed it out with the side of my hand. I cleared my throat and got comfortable on the grass. It was still a monster idea.

"Dear Dad." Too much of a whisper. I cleared my throat again and pitched my voice just above a normal conversation tone. Right out loud. "I've got all this junk in my head." Now I had the rhythm. The letter sounded even better when I read it out loud. "I'm really sorry you're dead. Boy, am I sorry."

Nuts! A car pulled up on the road just beyond the tree. A green Subaru, kicking up dust as it got closer. The car stopped. I stopped reading. A guy got out of the driver's side. He had on a white dress shirt with no tie and a pair of suit pants. He opened the passenger-side door for this old lady. She had on a nice print dress. Her hair was tied in a tight bun and her face was all red and puffy.

The two of them walked a few feet and stopped next to this grave that was covered with yellow flowers. They stood there and looked at the flowers. The man put his arm around the old woman's shoulder. She looked sad. He looked bored.

I shook my head. "Everything would have been so different if you hadn't decided to be such a hero." I'd lowered my voice, but it didn't matter. The people across the

129

road were staring at me like I was crazy. I dug a pack of Winstons out of my jeans pocket and lit a smoke with my lighter. I stared back at the people. The guy looked like he wanted to kill me. Like it was his private cemetery or something. Tough bananas. I had as much right to be there as he did.

"I just keep screwing up." A little louder. I couldn't help it. I sucked on my cigarette and plunged ahead. Just like I'd planned. "My other dads are doing their best to help me. I swear. They're the best guys in the world, but it's not working."

Whirrrrrrrrrrrr. Whirrrrrrrrrrrr. I almost jumped out of my skin. Just beyond the couple—across the road—this dumb-looking old fat guy in dirty overalls and no shirt was attacking the foliage around the outer fence of the cemetery with a Weed Eater. *Whirrrrrrrrrrrrrrrrrrrrr. Whirrrrrrrrrrrr.*

". . . treated me like a little kid." See it to the end. No matter what. "And Uncle Pat?" *Whirrrrrrrrrrrrrrrrr. Whirrrrr. Whirrrrrrrrrrrrrr.* ". . . fatter and fatter and balder and balder . . ." *Whirrrrrrr.* I read louder. I was almost shouting. "I saw Uncle Larry the other day." *Whirrrrrrr.* "Sometimes I just don't get Uncle Larry. There's a lot of stuff I don't get. The main thing I don't get is . . ." *Whirrrrrrrrr.*

I looked up again. The man and woman had left the graveside and moved to the edge of the road. They were gawking at me. Their noses were scrunched up like they had just smelled dirty feet. Too bad. I was on a mission.

"I don't know what makes me tick." My throat hurt, I

was reading so loud. "Everyone's waiting for me to screw up." *Whirrrrrrrrrr. Whirrrrrrrr.* Louder and louder and louder. *Whirrrrrrrrrrrrrrrr.*

"I wish I could be more like you."

The Weed Eater stopped. People just waking up in Oklahoma probably heard the last line I read. I mean, I was shouting as loud as I could. The couple across the road shook their heads. Then they hurried back to their car like they were afraid I might attack them or something. The old geezer with the Weed Eater sat down on a tombstone and lit a cigar. Sweat dripped off his fat old nose. The car roared out of the cemetery, leaving a cloud of dust. Mountain View was suddenly silent.

I felt like an idiot. I mean, what was I doing? Letters to dead people? Gimme a break. Then suddenly I didn't care. It was my idea. It was something I wanted to do. I turned my back to the old guy by the fence, sucked in a lot of air through my nose, straightened the letter in my lap, exhaled, and read on. "Maybe we'll meet someday. Like in heaven or somewhere." My voice was even. Purposeful. I finished my letter and then just sat there.

I know my real dad isn't underneath that tombstone in Mountain View. He's gone forever. Like ole Joe and Jane and little Jacob. But somehow sitting there next to that big slab of marble with my dad's name on it made me feel like he could hear me. Like maybe he knew what I felt. So I just sat.

Then I had another monster idea.

How about wrapping up the whole thing with a flourish? Yeah. Why not? I stood up and stretched my legs.

Then I pulled my lighter out of my pocket and set fire to the letter. The paper burned slowly, bright orange on the tip and black toward the center. The smoke smelled good in the warm morning air. I watched the ashes float toward the sky, upward toward heaven. Just before the flame reached my hand I dropped the smoldering paper on my real father's grave. It was a perfect moment.

Until the grass fire started.

The paper ignited the dry grass on the side of the grave. Then the fire spread. I started stomping on the flames with my Reeboks, but just as I would put some of it out, a little more would flare up.

Suddenly I was dancing around the grave like I was part of some primitive tribal ritual. Left, right, left, right, stomp, stomp, turn, stomp, turn, stomp. My Bulls cap fell off. Turn, stomp, turn, stomp. The fire spread to the high weeds beneath the tree. The smell of burning grass filled my nostrils. The fire was getting out of control. Where was the old guy with the Weed Eater?

What if the whole cemetery burned up? Turn, stomp, turn. What if the fire spread to the houses nearby? Turn, stomp. What if I burned up Bedford, Texas? How would I ever explain what I was doing out here?

I came out here to read a letter to my dead father. *Sure, Kenny, that makes a lot of sense. Everybody will buy that.* The fire spread to the grass by the roadside. Turn, stomp, turn, stomp. Unbelievable! Kenny Francis—God's greatest goofball. The kid who burned up the state of Texas.

CHAPTER 13

THE BELL RANG.

Everybody crammed their books and notebooks and pencils into their backpacks. The guys in the front row looked like sprinters waiting for the starting gun, ready to fly out the door by the time the echo of the bell stopped.

"I'll return your nine-week exams tomorrow," Mr. Abernathy said, talking quickly over the end-of-class noise. "We'll go over the test then. Most of you are going to be sorely disappointed. But what do you expect? Don't forget your homework assignment. Problems one through twenty on page ninety-eight. Just do the best you can with your limited abilities. All right, gentlemen. You're dismissed for the day."

Nobody had to be told twice.

"Jerk." A whisper escaped from the back of Mickey's throat. He slipped on his black raincoat and slung his backpack over his shoulder. "One week to Turkey Day. Geez, I can't wait to get home," he said out loud.

"Why? Are you planning to give all those San Antonio babes a thrill?" I said. "Red-Hot Holland, fresh from prep school. Lock up your daughters."

Mickey laughed. "Thanks, pal. You got it. The mighty Mick will be on the prowl."

I grinned and shook my head. The thought of Mickey Holland with a girl was funny.

Outside the rain gently pounded the windows, sending tiny rivers sliding down the windowpanes. Thanksgiving might be a week away, but inside Miller Hall it was summertime hot and stuffy. I loosened my tie and rolled up my sleeves.

"Let's head back to the dorm and shoot a little pool during free period," I said. "I just can't face problems one through twenty for a while. Particularly not with my limited abilities." I stuffed my algebra book in my backpack and draped the pack over my arm.

"You're on." Mickey headed for the back of the line filing out of Mr. Abernathy's class. I was right behind him.

"Mr. Francis."

I turned around.

Mr. Abernathy was sitting on the edge of his desk, dangling his legs in lazy circles. He had on a white turtleneck shirt under his blazer. His tan still looked like July. He motioned for me to come over.

"Uh-oh. I'll check you later," I said to Mickey. "The Big Cheese wants me."

"Good luck." Mickey slapped me on the arm. "I'll wait for you out front."

"Thanks."

From the look on Mr. Abernathy's face, I was heading for the heart of trouble city, which is always a possibility in my case.

Only two weeks earlier, I had put a major spin move on disaster and escaped in the nick of time. Disaster had just about had me. But I was saved at the last minute.

The grass fire around my father's grave had been raging out of control. I mean, the whole cemetery was going up in smoke and flames. I was stomping around, doing my dance, trying my damnedest to put out the blaze, when the old guy with the Weed Eater appeared with a fire extinguisher. He sprayed and I stomped and he stomped and I sprayed and together we gave disaster the slip. We put out the fire.

The old guy turned out to be pretty cool. All he said was, "Don't do this no more. I don't like it. The dead folks don't like it." That was it. He never asked who I was or what I was doing at the cemetery or anything. Just "Don't do this no more." I nodded and thanked him and ran all the way back to the dorm. Just in time for Saturday-morning breakfast.

I had dodged disaster, but now trouble was drawing a bead on me.

"I won't take much of your time, Mr. Francis."

I shrugged. I had plenty of time.

Abernathy looked at my loosened tie and rolled-up sleeves. He rolled his eyes. I might as well have stepped in a big cow patty. "I must say, I'm genuinely surprised you're still a student here."

I shrugged again.

"I've seen young men like you before. Accidents waiting to happen. After what you did with young Smith, I honestly thought you'd be out of here in a week. You've surprised me."

"I'm a surprising kind of guy."

"Don't be a wise guy, Mr. Francis. I'm trying to compliment you. It's not easy."

Why do so many adults hate to admit they're wrong? It's like after you turn twenty-one you're not supposed to make any mistakes. Like you get a quota of screwups, but you have to use them up before your twenty-first birthday. And then if you make a mistake, you can't admit it. Under no circumstances.

Mr. Abernathy let out a sigh. "Let me cut to the chase." This really was hard on him. "I graded your nine-week exam last night." He screwed up his face like he was constipated. "Solid B. One of the best papers in the class. I must admit I was shocked."

So was I. I mean, I'd been working my butt off to stay in Bedford, but a B on a major math test was unbelievable.

"I don't even think you cheated." Mr. Abernathy sounded disappointed. "In fact, I kept my eye on you throughout the test. It was a clean B. I thought you'd like to know. That's all."

It was killing him. Admitting he was wrong. Admitting he might have made a mistake about me. I loved it.

"Thanks."

"I still don't think you'll last the year," he said, desperate to get in the last word. "You don't have it in you. Losers like you always find a way to quit."

I squared my shoulders. "Not this time," I said. "I'm not just gonna finish the year. I'm gonna graduate from Bedford. Just like my father. You can take it to the bank."

I must have come on a little strong, because Mr. Abernathy leaned backward. He couldn't get used to teaching Texas gorillas. "Well, we'll see," he muttered. "We'll see. You're dismissed for now. I just thought you'd like to know about the exam."

I spun around and headed for the door. A B on my nine-week algebra test. Me. A B in Abernathy's class. Unbelievable. Even if the jerk himself delivered the news like the dork he was, a B was still a B. *Way to go, Kenny.*

This was a whole new experience for me. Success in school. Unheard of. I couldn't believe it. No teacher in my whole life had ever said anything nice to me. In third grade ole Miss Livingston had me stay after school one day. When everybody else had left she told me I was the child of the Devil and if I told anybody she said that, she'd swear I was lying.

Mickey was waiting by the outside door. "We might as well wait for Noah to show up with the ark," he said, indicating the rain. "We'll drown by the time we get back to the dorm."

Outside the gentle rain had turned into a torrent, pounding on the glass door.

"It'll be like taking a shower," I said, still giddy from my new academic success. "We'll swim back to the room, towel off, and hit the pool table. Nine-ball's my game, where I earned my fame. Get your money ready, I'm on a streak. I mean a *streak*." I was really feeling good.

Mickey smiled. "Abernathy must not have chewed on your ass much."

"Not a bit. The kid is on top of things. Let's hit the tables." The rain didn't scare me. I pushed open the door and led Mickey out into the storm.

The wind was whipping out of the west, and big raindrops blew past us horizontally, smashing against the buildings rather than falling to the ground. I had to lean into the wind to keep moving across the commons toward the dorm. At first I tried to cover my head with my backpack, but that was pointless, so I just slung the pack over my shoulder and pushed on, getting soaked.

I glanced back at Mickey. His black raincoat billowed out behind him like a giant cape. He looked like a drowning Batman.

I couldn't believe how dark it was. It was only about nine in the morning, but the sun had said *adiós* for the day. It was definitely time to seek shelter.

"This really sucks hard." Mickey was right behind me, but his voice sounded like it was coming from across the street.

"Well, anything that sucks can't be all bad," I said. Nothing could bother me. I was in a super mood. Big B.

Mickey didn't laugh. He was too wet.

The first one hit me on the back of the hand. It hurt. Not much, but some. Sleet. Nah, beyond sleet. Hail. Big hailstones pelted our retreat to the dorm. A couple hit me on the head. Little ice marbles. One caught me on the ear. Ouch.

"Oh, man!" Mickey's voice sounded farther away.

The hailstones got larger. I felt like some invisible giant was teed off at the planet and had started hurling frozen gravel at all of us. The bigger hailstones really hurt. Like getting hit with a rock.

Without saying anything, Mickey and I left the sidewalk and cut away from the path to the dorm, racing across the commons, sprinting to the chapel, which was only about twenty yards away. We found shelter under the Gothic overhang that fronted the entrance to the sanctuary.

I looked at Mickey and started laughing. His hair was plastered down over his forehead. His glasses were fogged over. He looked like some goofy insect that had just crawled out from under a wet rock.

"Man, this is strictly the pits." Mickey shook the water off his backpack. It was useless. Everything was soaked.

"It'll stop in a minute," I said, raising my voice to be heard over the sound of the hail pounding on the roof of the chapel.

"This is gettin' spooky," Mickey said. "Where is everybody?"

I looked out over the campus. He was right. There was nobody else around. No other students huddled in doorways or racing across the commons. Nobody. Just me and Mickey and the storm.

"Look at this," Mickey said. "It's like the middle of the night. Geez, it's dark. I can't even see the gym from here."

In the distance I could see lights glowing in the dorm windows. Mickey was right. It was midnight in the morning.

"This is so weird it's scary." Mickey wasn't laughing. "Something big's going on. I can just feel it."

I started yawning and swallowing to ease the popping sensation in my ears. Mickey said something else, but I couldn't hear him. Even though he was only about two feet away from me, the sound of the rain and hail smashing against the building drowned him out.

That and this dull roar from way off in the distance. At first the roar sounded like a train or maybe some kind of giant blowtorch, but as it got louder it seemed like a hundred jet airplanes all revving their engines at once.

My stomach tightened into a ball. Mickey and I looked at each other. His face was chalky. His lips were a tight line. He was right. Something major was going down.

I ran out from under the overhang and stood in the middle of the chapel courtyard. At first the rain was so strong I couldn't look up, but then the hail stopped and the rain slowed to a dull drizzle. Somehow it seemed even darker. I squinted and looked up at the sky, twirling around in the yard to see in every direction.

I saw them over the top of the gym. To the north.

"There they are," I yelled against the roar. "Over there! Look!"

Mickey stumbled out into the courtyard. "What are you talking about?" He looked where I was pointing.

"The tit clouds!" I shouted. "Just like you said! Look

at that! Hundreds of them! All over the sky! Look at 'em!''

Mickey grabbed my arm. "It's a tornado!" he yelled. "That's what that means. It must be heading this way. Listen!" The roar grew louder.

I whirled around and looked over the top of the chapel to the south. Nothing but thick black clouds. The darkness was like a blanket over the earth.

Mickey's lower lip came unglued. He was sniffing and bawling. He was scared out of his socks. He wiped his nose on the sleeve of his raincoat. "Come on, Kenny," he yelled. "We can't stand out here. Not next to the chapel. You know that's where the tornado will hit. They always hit churches. Come on, we've got to get out of here." He grabbed my shirt and started pulling me toward the dorm.

I shook free. I wasn't scared. Not a bit. Scared of nothing or nobody.

I was exhilarated. I whirled around and around across the courtyard, looking at the sky in all directions. "Where are you, you chicken tornado?" I yelled. "Let me see you. Show me what you've got! Give me your best shot! I'm not scared of you! Ya hear? Not scared a bit."

"Come on, Kenny. This is the real thing. This is—"

Suddenly the dark sky lit up. The heavens exploded with crackling lightning. Bright colors—yellows, greens, blues, purples. Bright, bright, exploding colors. All over the north Texas sky. It was better than the Fourth of July.

Mickey shrieked, "Run! We've got to get to a safe place!"

The wind almost knocked me down. I staggered back a couple of steps. My face was suddenly twisted like a Gothic gargoyle by the force of the wind. Behind me, the stained-glass window over the chapel entrance shattered. So did a pair of windows on the side of the building. A glass pane in the administration building, next to the chapel, blew out.

"Where are you?" I yelled, twirling around in the courtyard, my arms raised toward the sky. I felt the adrenaline shoot through my body. "Show me what you got! Give me your best shot! I'm not scared! Do ya hear?"

My voice died as the big roar hit. Ten times louder than before, like a thousand jet engines. Windows exploded all over the campus.

Mickey grabbed my arm. His grip was so tight it felt like his fingers were cutting into my flesh. He thrust his mouth next to my ear. "Don't be an idiot! We've got to get out of here now! We can't stay out here in the open. This is serious, man! Run! For God's sake, Kenny! Run!"

CHAPTER 14

WE RAN.

Mickey and I sprinted, scrambled, and dashed as fast as we could. Our dorm might as well have been somewhere over in Arkansas. The building was way too far away. So we ran across the back of the campus to Taylor Street, our legs pumping like pistons, our mouths sucking in air like it was in limited supply. Mickey's raincoat billowed behind him. My school tie flew over my shoulder like a tiny cape.

The roar got louder and louder.

Uncle Pat's Victorian house was just across Taylor Street. Just a matter of seconds when you're going a hundred miles an hour. When you're outrunning the wind.

We hit the porch at a full gallop, our arms flailing, water streaming off of us. *Bam! Bam! Bam!* I attacked the front door with my fists. "Uncle Pat! It's me! Kenny! Uncle Pat! Open up! It's a tornado! It's hit the school! Uncle

Pat! Open the door! We gotta get inside! Come on! Open up!''

After what seemed like forever and then some, the door opened. Just a few inches. There were no lights on in the house. Everything was dark, like a cave. The figure that opened the door was silhouetted against the continuous lightning that flashed around us like a neon sign. The figure groaned and staggered backward. The door opened wider.

Uncle Pat was drunk. At nine o'clock in the morning.

''Uncle Pat! Let us in! It's a tornado! I swear.''

Uncle Pat smiled this goofy smile, and Mickey and I pushed past him into the living room. '' 'S what I heard on the radio,'' Uncle Pat said. ''Before the damn radio died. 'S the end of the world as we know it. God must be furious at Bedford. Furious at us. Don't understand it. We never did anything to Him. At least not that I know of. Except—''

''We need to get away from the windows,'' Mickey said, ''so glass won't shatter on us. We need to get underneath something. In case the house collapses.''

'' 'S good thinking.'' Uncle Pat was really drunk. And contrary to popular opinion, drunks are anything but funny. They're exasperating. They're slow and stupid. Uncle Pat was trying to stand up straight, but he kept weaving around the living room. His face was pale and his eyes were sunk back in his head.

''How 'bout under the stairs?'' I said. ''In the hall closet.''

"Good idea." Uncle Pat turned and lurched toward the hallway. "That's a safe place. Come on."

Outside the roar grew louder. I pressed my palms against my ears. It didn't help much. The wind was blowing so hard all the windowpanes were rattling. The old house was creaking and moaning, whining about being assaulted by the wind.

Mickey crossed the room and lifted one of the windows. The wind whipped the curtains against his face. "It cuts the pressure," he said. "Might keep the house from exploding. It's worth a try."

I looked at Mickey with renewed admiration. The guy really did know a lot. "Good idea," I said.

In the hallway, Uncle Pat was tossing clothes and boots and boxes and hats out of the closet, clearing a place for us. The hallway looked like the tornado had already hit. "The damn electricity is out," he said. "Two hundred bucks a month and the stupid power company can't deliver electricity when you need it. Come on, get inside." He motioned toward the open closet door.

In the living room, the wind blew over a lamp. All three of us jumped when it shattered on the floor.

"Get in," Uncle Pat said, indicating the closet. "I'll be right back."

Mickey and I scrambled into the closet. Uncle Pat closed the door and disappeared. We tumbled into the back and waited, sitting scrunched together with our knees drawn up to our chests. Our hearts were pounding so loud I couldn't tell which was mine and which was Mickey's.

The closet smelled like an old jock strap. And it was dark. I mean *dark*. As dark as the night Uncle Larry and I went camping and I went to pee and couldn't find the tent.

Mickey and I were soaked, and every time we moved we made a squishing noise on the wooden floor. Our breath came in gasps. Gallons of adrenaline surged through my system, making it hard to sit still. Mickey's whole body was shaking. My ears were popping. I kept yawning and swallowing and rotating my jaw.

"So what happens now?" I asked.

"We pray the funnel doesn't hit the house," Mickey said. "If it does, we're dead." Outside, the wind howled through the house. Mickey's teeth were chattering. I hoped he wouldn't pee his pants like the last time he got scared. I decided not to raise the point.

"Dead at seventeen," Mickey said, delivering his own eulogy. "What a waste of talent. What a shame." Even though he was trying to be funny, Mickey was about to cry.

I reached over and frogged him on the arm. "We're not gonna die," I said. "We've still got too much harm to raise. You and me. Understand? It's not our time. That's all there is to it."

"Oh, how I wish," Mickey said.

The closet door opened, and Uncle Pat lurched through the entrance. He had a crystal tumbler in one hand and a couple of familiar red cans in the crook of his arm. "A little refreshment to pass the time," he said, handing each one of us a Coke. "God knows how long we may be here."

Uncle Pat's glass must have been pure bourbon. Suddenly the closet smelled like a distillery.

Uncle Pat plopped down at the other end of the closet. It was no easy matter. He was fat and drunk and trying to keep his bourbon from spilling. Finally he landed on the floor like a fish that had just been pulled out of the water. "Ah, what a day," he said. "And it's not even noon yet. Well, here's looking at you, kid. Even though I can't see ya. Either one of ya. Damn, it's dark in here."

Mickey and I opened our pop cans. Then we sat in the dark and sipped. Every time Uncle Pat let out a deep breath, the bourbon smell washed over us like a tidal wave.

I felt nauseous. Not scared. Nauseous.

"Well, you might as well know," Uncle Pat said after a while. "The batteries in the flashlight are dead. The batteries in the radio are dead. I've got some candles somewhere, but for the life of me I can't remember where. So I guess we'll just sit here and weather the storm." He chuckled. "Get it?"

It was a stupid line, and Mickey and I didn't laugh.

"Why didn't the TV weather people tell us this was coming?" I was surprised at the anger in my voice. "I mean, all those weather babes are always pointing at their big maps and showing you stupid low pressure in Montana and high pressure in Vermont. And the weather dudes with painted-on hair are always telling you to write in to get the station's tornado information kit. Seems like the best thing they could do would be to tell everybody the real thing was coming."

Uncle Pat hee-hawed. "The TV generation," he said. "It's not real if it's not on TV."

I really hoped we weren't gonna be trapped in a dark closet with Uncle Pat when he was in his cups and in his your-generation-is-shit mood. Talk about hell.

"They can't do it," Mickey said quietly. "The TV people just don't know. That's the truth. The best the meteorologists can do is warn that tornadoes are likely. Most of the time the colliding air masses work off their tension by producing thunderstorms. The weather people can't predict when the movement will provoke the spin of air that will kick off a twister. There's just no way. It's not their fault." Reciting encyclopedia knowledge had a calming effect on Mickey. Just like he told me. Facts leveled him out.

Uncle Pat said something, but the roar outside drowned him out. The house shook and creaked. Somewhere in the distance I heard a series of explosions. Instinctively I covered my head with my hands. Nobody tried to talk anymore. We just sat and sipped our drinks and waited to see what would happen, cringing in the dark with the house creaking and shaking all around us. I farted, but nobody could hear it with all the racket. I could feel Mickey shaking next to me. I hoped his bladder would hold. Every once in a while I could hear Uncle Pat rattling the ice in his glass. But mostly all I could hear was the roar and the rattling of the house.

Then suddenly silence hit like a bomb. Silence as in the total absence of noise. I could hear each breath Uncle Pat and Mickey drew. In and out. In and out. The roar was gone. The explosions had stopped. Nobody knew what to do next. So we just sat there. And sat and sat.

Until the phone rang in the hallway. Mickey squealed, and all three of us jumped like somebody stuck us with a cattle prod.

"Don't go answer it," Mickey whispered. "The phone's a conductor of electricity. You'll die if you answer it."

"Son," Uncle Pat said in his teacher voice, "life is full of dangers. Airplane crashes, car wrecks, having offspring. You name it. But to be honest, under the circumstances I'm willing to risk answering the telephone." He scrambled to his feet as best he could, grunting and straining and spilling the ice from his glass all over the closet floor. He opened the door and waddled down the hallway to the phone. He left the door open. The fresh air felt great.

I pressed my back against the closet wall and sucked in some deep breaths. I was so wet my shirt felt like it was fusing with my skin. My crotch was so damp it itched like crazy. Down the hallway I could hear Uncle Pat on the phone. I couldn't hear exactly what he was saying, but he sounded real calm.

Not knowing what to expect next was the strangest feeling. I mean, you live your whole life and you at least kinda know what each day is gonna be like and then all of a sudden, wham-bam, nothing is what it's supposed to be. There was no way to predict what was going to happen next. It could have been anything. It was weirdness in the extreme.

Uncle Pat's footsteps squeaked down the floorboards of the hallway. I looked up just as he thrust a lighted candle into the doorway. "Let's go, guys," he said in a surprisingly sober voice. "I found the candles in the kitchen. Come on. We've got work to do. Lots of work. I need both of you. We've got a major disaster on our hands. Apparently we just lived through the worst tornado that ever hit north Texas. Possibly one of the worst in American history. The funnel must have just missed us. It's hit the town in spades. Houses are crushed. People are hurt. We need every able-bodied man to help. That means you two. Let's go."

Mickey and I scrambled out of the closet and stood in the hallway, dripping water on the floorboards. Uncle Pat stood in front of us, holding the candle at his side. Suddenly he didn't seem drunk at all. He seemed like a sergeant giving orders to his platoon. "First," he said, "I'm gonna give each one of you a dry sweatshirt. You look like drowned rats. I can't help you with the pants. Geez, I could fit both of you in one pair of mine. How did I get so big? Well, no matter. Later on there'll be time for you to get back to the dorm and change. Right now we've got to get to work. Apparently the damage is incredible. All over town. The Red Cross is setting up a shelter in our gym. I talked to Mr. Wellington and one of the Red Cross workers on the phone. I volunteered the three of us for an assignment, so we need to get going."

"What kind of an assignment?"

Uncle Pat smiled. "I think you'll go for it, Kenny," he said. "It calls for some of your best traits. Basically, I need strength and courage. There's folks out there that need our help. Come on, let's saddle up and ride.''

"Oh, man!" Mickey's voice went up about ten octaves. He was almost shrieking. "We can't go out there right after a tornado! That's nuts. Do you know what—"

I put my arm around Mickey's wet shoulder and pulled him close to me. "Save it for when we get back," I said in the calmest voice that had come out of my mouth in a long, long time. "Like the man said, it's time to ride."

CHAPTER 15

TWO MINUTES AFTER WE LEFT UNCLE PAT'S HOUSE I KNEW WHY MICKEY WAS SCARED TO GO OUT. The tornado had changed everything. Turned the world upside down.

The area around the campus looked like a war zone. Beirut, Belfast, Bedford. Houses were caved in like some clumsy giant had stepped on them, squeezing the insides out like a tube of toothpaste, scattering sofas and tables and chairs and lamps and stuff over the yards and driveways. Other houses were suddenly roofless—looking unnatural and uncomfortable, like a bald guy whose toupee has been snatched off his head.

Trees had been uprooted and flung across streets and sidewalks. Cars had been rearranged up and down the street at odd angles, turned upside down, and scattered over lawns. All the tires had blown out. Nightmare city.

Mickey and Uncle Pat and I walked down Taylor Street, circling the edge of the Bedford campus. There wasn't any particular reason to move slowly, except we couldn't stop ourselves from gawking at the wreckage. All three of us moved cautiously, like we expected a lion to jump out of the bushes at any minute.

We were a funny-looking trio. I had on one of Uncle Pat's sweatshirts, a blue one with JUST DO IT on the front in red and white letters. The thing hung down to my knees. I had retrieved my black Bulls cap from my backpack and had it on backward. Who cared how it looked? It was my hat and it just felt better that way.

Mickey had on a white sweatshirt that would have covered a small building. The big black letters across the front read WILL WORK FOR SEX. A seriously stupid joke under the circumstances. Unfortunately, it was the only other sweatshirt Uncle Pat had. Mickey had on his black raincoat, which kept billowing out behind him like Batman's cape.

Uncle Pat still had on a white dress shirt and tie, but the tie was undone and his shirttail had come out in the back. What little hair he had left stuck up in the air in scattered tufts that looked like little horns.

The rain continued to fall in a slow drizzle from a mustard-colored sky. The sun had vanished. The air was filled with a gassy odor, like Mother Nature had just cut the world's record fart.

I had this feeling that any minute I'd roll over and wake up and think, *Wow. What a weird dream. This tornado hit Bedford and wrecked everything, and Uncle Pat and*

Mickey and I had to go out and help people. What a goofy dream!

Only I didn't wake up. The terrible trio just kept waltzing across the weird planet. Walking across a nightmare.

Everything was quiet, like the whole world was holding its breath. A couple of times we saw some people down the block. Wandering around, crying, holding each other. They all moved like zombies. We just kept walking, circling the uprooted trees and overturned cars. Nobody had anything to say.

Finally the silence got to me. "Can you believe this?" I said.

"It's worse than anything I ever read about," Mickey said. "Not one book I ever read described what this would be like. Not one. This is the worst day of my life. No exceptions."

I exhaled a deep breath. "Me too."

"It's like a giant vacuum cleaner hit the place," Mickey said. "The nozzle on the ground, the tank in the clouds. The thing just scoured the ground, smashing everything it couldn't suck up. Man, this is awful."

"It's the worst thing ever."

"It's like Vietnam," Uncle Pat mumbled. "Nothing like it should be."

Mickey and I just looked at each other.

The terrible trio shuffled on down the street.

"So where are we going?" I said after a while. I don't like surprises.

"A couple more blocks," Uncle Pat said. "At least I think it is. Everything looks so different. I'm not even sure where we are. We're heading for the End of the Line. You know, the little shopping area they made out of the train depot. The Red Cross guy said he thinks there may be some people inside the arcade. He wants us to check on them. He thinks the funnel passed right over it."

I remembered the place from the night Uncle Larry and I took a walk before Uncle Pat served dinner. The place with all the glass. I didn't want to think about it.

Mickey quickened his pace to keep up with me. "I hope everybody's okay," he said. "I mean, I hope nobody is hurt or bleeding or anything. I flunked my CPR class. Geez. I hope somebody opened the windows before the funnel hit. That's real important." Mickey's voice had this hoarse, flat quality to it, like all his emotions had gone on a quick vacation.

"What are you talking about?"

"The windows. The air pressure. Don't you get it?" Just the facts. It was Mickey's way of dealing with things. I had to admit, it had a certain logic to it. "That's the answer to the mystery."

"Mickey, what in the world . . . ?"

"That's why tornadoes always smash churches instead of saloons. Churches are only open on Sunday for worship services. Then they're closed up tight during the week. All the doors and windows are closed. Think about it. But old-timey saloons had doors that were nothing but light, swinging panels of wood. All the windows were open if it was hot. So if the twister hit on, say, a Wednesday, then when the funnel dropped over a saloon, the air pressure inside could quickly equalize with the suddenly lowered

155

pressure outside. When the funnel found a church, the building was sealed, the pressure built up real fast, and the roof blew off or the walls blew down. How about that?"

"That's amazing," I said. "You're the smartest guy I ever met. No kidding. That's really amazing."

Mickey took a mock bow. "You would have figured it out eventually," he said.

"Save some of that brain power, guys," Uncle Pat said. "I think we're gonna need it. Look over there."

I looked up. Then I wished I hadn't. It was awful.

The End of the Line had hit the end of the line. The whole little shopping area had been trashed. When Uncle Larry and I had hiked past the place, everything had been so neat, so prim and proper, so orderly.

Now it was garbage. Everything had gone kaboom. The windows in the front of the remodeled depot had all blown out. Shattered glass glistened all over the sidewalk like a zillion diamonds in the mustard-colored light.

A humongous oak tree had been tossed into the center of the arcade, smashing through the roof. A blue Jeep Cherokee had been tossed in on top of the tree. It was like a crazy salad.

"Hello! Hello!" Uncle Pat called as we approached. "We've come to help you. The Red Cross has set up a shelter at the Bedford Academy gymnasium. That's only about a mile from here. There are doctors and nurses there. And blankets and emergency phones. We've come to take you there. Hello!"

Nobody answered.

"What if they're dead?" Mickey whispered. "What if

there are dead people in there? I've never even seen a dead body. What are we gonna do if they're all dead? I'm not sure I can take that. You know what I'm saying?''

"Shhh.'' I looked at Mickey. "It'll be okay.'' I sounded like I saw dead people every day. Forget that. I'd never seen a dead body in my whole life. But I still wasn't scared. No way.

We walked into the arcade, our sneakers crunching on the shattered glass. All the stuffed clowns from the Dining Car were blown and scattered across the arcade. Some were missing their heads, or their arms, or their legs.

"Hello! Is there anybody here?''

The smell of coffee was everywhere. Java River had been hit hard. The little espresso shop was a major disaster area. As we moved into the arcade I could see busted pipes in the back of the shop spewing water. I could see the brightly colored kettles and fancy coffee cups scattered all over the carpeted floor. The twister had overturned the counter and blown the chairs and tables all over the place. And everywhere there were battered, limbless, grinning clowns.

Then I saw a human face.

The face belonged to a woman. She was maybe in her mid-forties, with speckled gray hair and pasty skin. Her right eye was coated with blackish caked blood from a cut on her forehead. A couple of her front teeth were missing. The other teeth were stained pink with more blood. I had no idea blood came in so many different colors.

"Help us! Please help us!'' The woman was alive. She was standing in front of the door of the espresso bar, pounding on the thick glass. "I can't get the door open!" Her voice was a high-pitched shriek. "There are other people here. Some of them are hurt. My granddaughter's here. She's just a little girl. Please help us!"

"We're on our way!" Uncle Pat started moving the debris in front of the door. "Hang on! We're coming!"

Mickey and I grabbed the branches of the tree that blocked the doorway. Uncle Pat squatted beside us, and we all pushed and heaved and strained until the tree rolled a couple of feet away from the door.

Uncle Pat opened the door and slipped into the building. The woman collapsed in his arms. Then she came unglued, wailing and sobbing and rocking her body back and forth.

"She's in shock," Uncle Pat said quietly. "Bless her heart. What an ordeal." He patted her on the back. "Put your raincoat over her, Mickey. We need to keep her warm."

Mickey tore off his coat. "Here," he said, draping the raincoat over the woman's shoulders. "Don't cry. We're here to help you." His voice was quivering.

"The others. Please help them."

While Uncle Pat guided the woman into the arcade hallway, Mickey and I fanned out over Java River.

"Over here." It was dark, and at first I couldn't tell where the voice came from.

"There." Mickey pointed. "In the corner. Behind that overturned table."

It was a pair of old guys. I mean, old guys. White hair,

wrinkled faces, stooped shoulders. One of them, a short man with a big veiny nose, was lying on the wet carpet, the bottom part of his body twisted at a funny angle. His blue suit was soaking wet. The other guy, a silver-headed dude wearing a green shirt and rainbow-colored suspenders, sat next to his buddy. They were holding hands.

"It's about time you got here," Silver Hair snapped. "Poor Elmer's broke his leg. We need an ambulance. And a stretcher. He can't move."

"I'm all right," Elmer said, rolling over on his side. "I took worse in the war. Fought my way up the beaches of Normandy. Me and Walt here. We was just a couple of Bedford boys. We was with the first American unit to enter Germany. We kicked the Krauts' butts. I guarantee you that. Naw, a broken leg ain't nothing to me. I took a bullet in my backside in forty-four. That hurt a lot worse than this. I jest can't move my dad-blamed leg. That's all. Don't y'all mind me."

"Hush, you old fool," Walt said. "This ain't the Big War. You ain't no shiny-faced GI. You hear me? You've gone and busted your leg. Now be still."

"How can we help?" Mickey knelt down beside Elmer.

"We can't move him," Walt said. "Not without a stretcher. We got to get more help." He leaned his back against the overturned table, clearly glad to have someone to share his burden. "Me and Elmer come here every morning. Every morning right at nine. We have our coffee and remember stuff. Jest me and him. We didn't have no idea this was gonna happen. Worst storm I ever saw. First was this big roar. Like German artillery. Then all the glass started breakin' and the building started shakin'. I tell you, it was something awful.''

I stood up and looked around the wrecked coffee bar. I could almost feel the presence of other people in the place. I was right. A young guy with a bushy moustache was sitting on the floor, resting his back against the brick wall. A little girl sat in his lap. The guy had on a white shirt and a brown apron with JAVA RIVER printed on the front. The girl was about five. She had on a pretty red dress. She was soaking wet, her hair plastered down on her forehead. The guy looked like death warmed over. His skin was a yellowish color and he was staring off into space, absentmindedly stroking the girl's hair. He was really on Mars.

I had the feeling the little girl was taking care of the Java River guy. Talking to him and laughing and trying to keep his mind off what was happening.

I sidestepped a couple of overturned chairs and approached them. ''Hi. How's it going?'' I mean, what else could you say?

''We're fine,'' the little girl said, like she was in the middle of a Sunday-afternoon tea party. ''Todd's my friend. He fixes me special spice tea when Grandma brings me here. Todd fell down and bumped his head. When the tree fell outside. It made a terrible noise. We were all scared. But we're not scared now. Not since you got here. We knew you'd come. My grandma told us. So we're not scared.''

Todd looked scared.

"How you doin', man?" I crouched down next to the guy.

His eyelids fluttered. "Okay, I think. I took a real shot on the head. Probably a concussion or something. I'll be okay."

I reached out and squeezed his shoulder. "We'll get you over to the Bedford gym," I said. "They'll have blankets and dry clothes and stuff. You guys are soaked. I bet there'll be a doctor there. You look like you could use some help."

The guy nodded his head. The motion seemed to really hurt.

"Can you walk?"

"I think so. Maybe with a little help."

"You got it. Come on." I took his hand and helped Todd to his feet. He was pretty shaky.

"Thanks, darling," he said to the little girl. "I couldn't have made it without you."

The little girl beamed. "My name's Ginger," she said to me. What's your name?"

"Kenny," I said. "It's nice to meet you."

She took my hand. Tornadoes make instant friends.

We got Ginger and her grandma and Todd and Walt together by the door, where we held a conference. Todd told us that Java River was the only arcade shop open that early. He had been minding the coffee shop by himself, he said, and he assured us they had been the only people in the building when the twister hit. When he finished talking he looked like he might throw up.

"The Red Cross people are set up in our gym," Uncle

Pat said. "We'll take you there. Get you some help. I know this has been a terrible experience for all of you."

"Elmer can't walk," Walt said. "His leg's broke. He's a tough old nut, but he ain't that tough."

"I'll stay with him," Mickey said quietly. "I don't mind staying. I'll just sit and keep him company. It's no big deal."

My admiration for Mickey was growing by the minute. "Okay, Mick," I said. "I'll help these folks get to the gym and then I'll come back with reinforcements. I'll get an ambulance and we'll get him to a hospital."

Mickey gave me the thumbs-up sign. "Elmer and I will be here," he said. "We're sure not going anywhere."

I smiled.

Mickey headed for the back of the coffee bar, and by the time Uncle Pat and I ushered the other people out of Java River, Mickey and Elmer were yukking it up like a pair of old war buddies. Elmer had to be in pain, but he wasn't letting it show. He was one tough old guy.

I gave Mickey a goodbye wave and helped Todd down the hallway. "This is a little harder than I thought," Todd said in a flat voice. "But I can walk."

That was only partly true. He could take a few steps, then stop. Like he had forgotten to turn off the stove or something. Then he'd start up again.

Up ahead, Uncle Pat took Ginger's hand and steered her grandmother by the elbow. Walt walked a couple of steps behind, shuffling his feet and mumbling to himself. I took Todd's arm, and we brought up the rear.

We inched our way out of the arcade, our feet crunching

on the broken glass. Everybody walked slowly, like we had all just learned how. I wanted to go faster so I could get to the gym and get some help for Mickey and old Elmer. I mean, both of them must have been spooked—stuck in the trashed coffee bar. I wanted to get help as soon as possible.

Crippled turtles could have sped past our little parade. It was one step at a time. Ginger's grandma was hurt, Walt was old, and Todd was disoriented. And Uncle Pat weighed more than the offensive line of the Dallas Cowboys. None of this lent itself to sprinting to the finish line.

Besides, it was hard to sell anybody on a stroll across a town that's just been blown to bits by a tornado. It's not a fun place to be. It's spooky. The sky is yellow, everything stinks, nothing is where it should be. Houses are smashed. Cars are on their sides, trees are sprawled across the streets. Nobody wants to walk through hell. All you want to do is jump in bed and pull the covers over your head.

The gym was maybe a mile away. After a while, it seemed like the gym was in Montana. One step at a time. I really felt sorry for Mickey.

It was getting darker. With all the electricity out, there were no streetlights or lights from any of the houses. Nothing but the eerie mustard glow in the tornado sky.

I could see the tiled roof of the gym in the distance. *Hang in there, Mickey. Just a few more minutes.*

The drizzle picked up. I hoped that didn't mean the funnel might come back. I mean, when does this stuff end? How do you know it's over?

Like a bunch of exhausted marathon runners, we finally

stumbled across the finish line—the door to the Bedford gym. All of us—me and Uncle Pat and Ginger and Grandma and Todd and Walt—shook hands and hugged. We had made it across the wasteland into the safety of the gym.

Only I wasn't finished. Mickey and Elmer were still out there. I had to get help and get back to the End of the Line.

CHAPTER 16

HOME OF THE BULLDOGS.

The blue-and-white banner that hung over the gymnasium scoreboard was faded and frayed. The sign had seen better days. So had the gym.

The home of the Bulldogs had been built back in the fifties, when sunken living rooms were the big deal. Bedford wound up with a sunken gym. You walked in at the top, and the permanent bleachers and concrete steps, which were only on one side, led down to the shiny wooden playing floor below.

Across the floor were the opposing benches and the scorekeepers' table and the frayed banner over the scoreboard flanked by a couple of mammoth blue-and-white signs on the wall. Signs like BEDFORD BULLDOGS, 5-A DISTRICT CHAMPS, 1958 followed by a list of all the guys that played on the team. BEDFORD ACADEMY, 5-A DISTRICT FOOTBALL

My real dad and Uncle Pat's names were on that list. Along with Bobby Kinkaid's name. State champs. I didn't have time to think about it.

Uncle Pat and I shepherded our little group through the entrance door into the top part of the gym, and everybody sucked in a surprised collective breath at the sight of the chaos on the floor below.

The place throbbed like a county fair. Activity everywhere. The regular electricity was out, and the lights run by the auxiliary generator were flickering and making everyone's skin look slightly purple.

Someone had set up a row of cots underneath the basketball backboard. A bunch of people were lying on the cots, their faces or arms or legs wrapped in bandages. Blood was in evidence everywhere. A woman in a nurse's uniform was taping gauze to an overalled farmer's cheek. Three women sat huddled together on one cot, their arms around each other, bawling their eyes out.

There was a pair of card tables in the far corner with a Red Cross sign hanging in front of them. Two frazzled-looking women wearing Red Cross armbands sat behind the tables marking stuff on clipboards, thumbing through papers, and talking to the triple rows of people lined up in front of them. Everybody was gesturing and talking with their hands. Some people were shouting and I don't think they even knew it.

Other people milled around the gym floor, looking lost and dazed, going nowhere, just needing to move. Some of them were wrapped in army blankets, looking like they were playing Indian. Periodically they would spot somebody they knew and go up to them and embrace them and pat them on the back and talk to them in low voices.

There were women with rollers in their hair, men in coats and ties, guys in overalls and T-shirts, little kids clinging to their moms' legs or racing around the gym like it was recess.

I spotted a group of Bedford students in the corner of the bleachers, everybody talking at once. I saw Chad and Andy and Gentle Ben. Everybody was mega-excited, like they were on speed or something. Lots of hand gestures. Lots of loud voices. Lots of backward baseball caps. Nobody felt preppy.

Most of the people in the gym were wet, their hair plastered down on their foreheads, their shirts stuck to their skin. No one seemed to care. Being damp was the least of their worries.

A woman in a burnt-orange sweatshirt was serving coffee in Styrofoam cups from a pair of urns behind the scorer's table. The smell of fresh coffee mixed with the scent of ancient sneakers and body odor.

Uncle Pat and I led our charges to the nurses' station under the backboard. One of the nurses took Todd over to a cot and helped him lie down. He looked terrible. He tried to wave to me, but his arm flopped around like a fish somebody had just reeled in—totally out of control.

We parked Ginger and Grandma and Walt with the other Red Cross people. Grandma started to cry with relief.

Just before Uncle Pat and I took off, old Walt gently

took my arm. "I know I'm an ancient windbag," he said, "but dad-burn it, you remind me of this young private in our outfit. Back at Normandy. Hell of a man. He was from Georgia or somewhere down South, just a good ole country boy. He was cool and calm in the face of the enemy. Nothin' bothered him. You two are just alike. You ain't scared a whit. Neither one of you scared of anything. No sir."

I nodded my thanks and started pulling away, anxious to find somebody to go back with me to relieve Mickey and get poor Elmer to a hospital. "So what happened to him?" I asked, just to be polite.

"He got killed," Walt said. "That ole Georgia boy took a bullet the day we landed. A real shame. But you two is just alike. Well, thanks for all you done. I 'preciate it. You get on back there now and look after Elmer. He's a good man. Go on now, you hear?"

"Thanks." I smiled.

Uncle Pat had wandered off under the backboard. I needed his help, but all of a sudden he looked feeble. Exhausted. He looked like he had aged ten years in the last ten minutes. His face was chalky and he walked like he had a load in his pants.

When I caught up with him, he managed a weak smile. "I'm proud of you, Kenny," he said in a low voice. "This has really been a nightmare. I know Dickie would have been real proud. You're all right, kid."

I nodded. I didn't know what else to do. I mean, I hadn't really done all that much. Just walked a few people from the End of the Line to the gym. Sure, there had been a tornado and everything, and some of the people were pretty banged up. But I wasn't exactly Arnold Schwarzenegger. And I still had to locate some help for Mickey and old Elmer.

Uncle Pat looked too beat to be of much help, so I threaded my way through the crowd on the gym floor, searching for somebody. The whole gym was full of anguish. Fearful voices. Terrified voices. The echoes of despair.

"The whole garage was smashed," one guy said. "Crushed to the ground. Car and all. Best car I ever owned. Completely smashed."

"No. We haven't seen her since the twister hit. I'm worried sick. I don't know where she could be." That was a woman in a faded print dress, wringing her hands.

"Twenty years we scrimped and saved for that house. And now it's gone." A middle-aged guy in a purple polo shirt, fighting back the tears. "Everything's gone."

"They're sayin' none of the insurance companies will pay," a guy in a Kmart suit said. "They say there's a clause in the fine print. They don't have to pay nobody nothing. It just don't seem fair."

"The whole town looks like it's been bombed," an old lady offered to no one in particular.

"Does this mean we're gonna be street people?" a young woman with a baby on her hip asked. "Are we gonna live like those smelly people under the viaduct off the LBJ Freeway in Dallas?"

The young guy with her studied the banners over the scoreboard and didn't say a word.

"It's God's will, I reckon," a farmer in overalls said to me as I walked past him. "Yeah, that's it. God's will."

I finally spotted a Texas state trooper leaning against the scorer's table. He was a burly guy with stubble on his chin. His uniform shirt was drenched with sweat and rain. He was sipping coffee out of a Styrofoam cup while he talked to a bald guy wearing a Red Cross armband.

"It's brought out the looters," the trooper said to his buddy as I approached the table. "The Raven Glen rednecks are swarming all over the place. We got some National Guard help, but man, we're all too busy searching the rubble for survivors. I've been out there since the twister hit. But there's only so much a man can do. We'll dig for about fifteen minutes and then blow the whistle for silence. Listen for anybody that might be trapped underneath all that crap. I don't see how they make it. Buried under bricks and heavy lumber. Seems like it'd crush you. But we've found three folks that way, still alive. It's a miracle. This has got to be the worst twister in Texas history. Got to be."

"Excuse me," I said, moving next to the trooper, "I need some help. There's an old man with a broken leg trapped inside the End of the Line. Over in the Castle Street development. In the Java River coffee shop. My friend's staying with him, but they're out there all alone and the old man is really hurt. He needs a stretcher and an ambulance. He needs to be in a hospital."

The trooper smiled at me and shook his head. "Yeah, I know the place. I know just where you're talking about. Thanks, kid. But let me tell you, ambulances are in short supply. As in there just aren't any." He ran his hand over his stubble and shook his head, looking momentarily overwhelmed by everything that had to be done.

"No. You don't understand," I said. "The old guy's leg is all twisted and—"

The cop exhaled and winked at me. "I tell you what I'll do," he said. "I'll round up a couple of the National Guard fellows and get them to use one of their Jeeps. They can help carry the guy out. I know it's not an ambulance, but it's probably the best we're gonna be able to do. Okay?"

I didn't realize I had been holding my breath. Suddenly I exhaled with a loud whoosh. "Cool." I said. "That'd be great. I'll head back over there and tell them you guys are on the way. I know Mickey's about to freak. Thanks."

"Thank you," the Red Cross guy said. "We need all the folks like you we can find."

"You get on over there," the trooper said. "The Guardsmen will be there as soon as they can. I promise."

"Okay." I nodded and started back across the gym floor, weaving my way through the crowd. Underneath the far backboard, I saw Todd sitting up on his cot, sipping some coffee. The color had returned to his face. Little Ginger sat at the foot of the cot talking ninety miles an hour, looking after her friend. It was a cute scene, a happy ending. I liked it.

"Kenny, man. Way to go!" Bobby Adams, a pimply-faced guy from my math class, came up behind me and threw his arm around my shoulder. "We heard what you and Mouse did. Way to go!"

I must have looked startled. Bobby pulled his arm back.

"We heard you guys saved a whole bunch of people," he said. "You guys are a couple of heroes. Way to go! Man, the tornado was unbelievable. Me and Larry Harris and Chad Jones had just left Mr. Abernathy's class, and we were almost back to the dorm. Boy, I knew something was bad wrong, you know what I mean?"

Adrenaline had seized Bobby's tongue.

"The way the sky looked. So then we heard this roar. Of course, I knew right then what it was. Anyway, all of us got in the basement of the dorm. Unbelievable. Everything was blowin' and goin'. Radical to the max. Really awesome."

The guy had never spoken to me before. Everyone had a tale to tell. Where were you when the Texas twister hit?

"Have you heard the latest?" Bobby asked.

I shrugged.

"They've got this thing," Bobby said. "It's like the Richter scale, you know, for earthquakes. It's called the Fujita-Pearson Tornado Intensity Scale."

It seemed like Bobby liked facts, just like Mickey.

"It goes from F-One, which is moderate, you know, a hundred miles an hour or something, to F-Five, which would pretty much be the end of the world. The twister that just hit? Try this. Over two hundred miles an hour. An

F-Four. Can you believe that? An F-Four? We were in the middle of an F-Four tornado! Is that just totally awesome or what?''

"Yeah. That's something." I grinned. It wasn't funny or anything, but the fact was that being in a tornado was exciting. Everybody was on an excitement high or something.

"The campus is okay," Bobby rattled on. "But the houses around the school? Wow. Most of them look like they were bombed. We won't have class tomorrow. The whole school will be closed. Thank God. Who wants to see their algebra test?''

I suddenly remembered what Mr. Abernathy had told me about my own exam earlier that day. Solid B. The test seemed like such a trivial matter now. The conversation with Mr. Abernathy seemed like something that took place a long, long time ago. Like maybe in a previous lifetime.

"Listen, man, I got to go," I said. "Mickey's still out there with this old guy who's got a busted leg. They're waiting for me. Hey, go with me. Maybe we can help the National Guard guys get the old man out. Come on. We can use your help."

Bobby took a step backward. "I dunno, man. You're really not supposed to go out there. After a tornado and all. You know, power lines and gas leaks and stuff like that." He licked his lips, which apparently had suddenly turned into a desert. "You ought to let the authorities take care of everything now. You know what I'm saying?''

Actually, I didn't. And I didn't have any more time for Bobby Adams. I didn't even have time to think about Bobby Adams. "Suit yourself," I said. "But I gotta go."

"Don't be such a hero," Bobby said, trying to get in the last word.

I shrugged. "I'll see you around," I said as I headed back into the crowd.

I waved to Uncle Pat, who had found a seat in the bleachers. He had a grayish olive blanket wrapped around his shoulders. He looked like he was about a hundred and ten years old. He waved back, slowly, as though it took a lot of effort.

Taking the bleacher steps two at a time, I sprinted to the top of the gym and hit the exit door at a full gallop. Outside, the mustard sky had lightened a little, and the drizzle had stopped. Maybe the whole tornado thing was over. One more job and my part was over for sure.

Head back to the End of the Line and tell Mickey and old Elmer to hang on, the cavalry was coming. Just like in the movies. One more job and my part was finished. Piece of cake.

CHAPTER 17

AS SOON AS I CLEARED THE GYM DOOR, I BROKE INTO A TROT. I was getting worried about poor Mickey. He had been stuck in Java River with old Elmer for what seemed like hours. Just the two of them, waiting for help in the dark and damp tornado fallout. Waiting for me.

So I took up jogging.

The world outside the gym was still sci-fi city. An eerie reddish hue hung over Bedford. A red world with a sickly yellow sky.

Bobby Adams had been right. The residential neighborhood that flanked the campus was a wasteland. Everything was trashed. There was a nasty stench clinging to the air.

Tiny fires had broken out in the rubble that used to be people's homes. The glow helped illuminate the reddish twilight. Nothing moved. No breeze. No noise. Just stillness.

Aaaagghhh! I jumped back just before I stepped on a dead dog lying on the sidewalk. A big German shepherd. The poor thing was all mangled. His organs had exploded, ripping open his stomach, scattering blood and guts all over the sidewalk. His eyes stared up at me like they were looking for help.

I spun around and sprinted to the other side of the street to avoid the thing. I wanted to get as far away from that dog as I could. I was breathing hard. It wasn't from the jogging.

I sprinted another block. Then I gave out. I mean, a pack of Winstons a day had not exactly left me in marathon shape. So I walked.

Then I stopped.

A red Ford Probe had turned over in someone's yard and come to rest on its side. From the looks of things, the driver had gotten out of the car and tried to reach the house. The poor guy was probably looking for shelter when the funnel hit. He never made it.

The tornado did its number and the guy wound up dead in the yard. I could tell he was dead. I mean, I didn't need to look for a pulse or anything like that.

I don't know why I did it. Curiosity, I guess. Morbid curiosity. Or stupidity. Knowing me, it was probably both. I went over to look at the body. It was gross. There was blood all over everything. All over the guy's white turtleneck, all over the sidewalk, all over the grass. Red-black blood in puddles and patches everywhere.

The really gross part was that as I walked up the front walk I realized the guy's left arm had been ripped off his body. I swear. All these bloody tendons and arteries or whatever spilled out of the hole where the guy's arm used to be.

I gagged. Sweat formed in my pits and trickled down my rib cage. I thought I was gonna puke right there.

I walked up to the body and looked at it. Oh, man, oh, man, oh, man! The guy looked just like Mr. Abernathy, my math teacher. I mean, they were both about the same age, and both had on turtlenecks. It was really creepy.

The dead guy's eyes were open and his mouth was curled in a snarl. A piece of wood, a single picket off a white picket fence, had been driven through his chest by the wind. He looked like a vampire who had been stabbed in the heart with a stake. I leaned over and vomited all over the sidewalk. I couldn't help myself.

This isn't happening. This is some kind of a stupid dream. Wake up, Kenny. None of this is real.

It was real, and the guy was dead.

Close his eyes. That's what they always do in the movies. Just push 'em shut.

No way, José. I wasn't about to touch a dead body. Not this one or any other one. Instead, I backed out of the yard, keeping my eyes on the Mr. Abernathy look-alike. My stomach rock-and-rolled all over the inside of my body. I was gasping for air, like the oxygen on the planet had suddenly run short. My skin felt prickly. I wanted to turn around and run.

You're scared. Scared of a dead body. Scared like some snotty-nosed little kid. You want to run home to your mommy.

I'm not scared of anything or anybody. You can take that to the bank. So I didn't run away from the yard and the body. I walked away quickly. There's a difference. Honest.

You're scared, you chicken.

I wasn't scared. I was nervous. Or something like that. Shook up, maybe. Rattled. But not scared.

I jogged again. Slowly at first. Then faster. Actually, I ran about a block. It felt great. Before my breath ran out.

As I got close to the railroad crossing, I was greeted by the first noise I had heard since I left the gym. I guess I hadn't noticed it before. You know, with the dead body and everything. Anyway, something must have blown across the tracks and shorted out the signal, because the signal bell was clanging. The red lights flashed on and off, and the guard rail went up and down. There were no trains. *Clang! Clang! Clang!* The noise wouldn't stop. I wished somebody would switch it off.

I hurried on past the crossing and ran down a side street that came out a block from the End of the Line. I could still hear the stupid, mindless clanging in the distance. Like it was following me or something.

The sight of the End of the Line revived my spirits a little. I couldn't do anything about the dog or the dead guy, but at least I could help Mickey. I jogged across the street and crunched my way into the old depot. The place still reeked of coffee, and the thousand clowns were still grinning their stupid heads off.

I squeezed past the tree in the arcade entrance and through the door of Java River. Everything looked the same. The pipes were still spewing water like Niagara Falls. Tables and chairs were still turned over, kettles and junk scattered everywhere, the counter turned on its side.

Elmer was still behind the counter, propped up in the corner, his leg still twisted at this gross angle. The old man waved when he saw me coming through the door. I waved back. Everything was the same.

Except Mickey was gone.

"Geez, man. How's it going?" I squatted down beside Elmer.

The old man was major pale. "Well, I reckon I've had better days." He managed a smile. "But all things considered, I'm doing right well. If I sit up like this, I don't hardly feel my leg."

Elmer was one tough old bird. No whining. No complaining. Just doing right well.

"You don't look so hot yourself, son," Elmer said.

I drew in a deep breath. "It's okay," I said. "Except I just saw this body. A guy that looked just like my math teacher. He . . . got killed in the tornado. I just stumbled across him. . . . He looked . . . really gross. You know what I mean?"

Elmer drew his lips into a thin line and nodded. "I know what you mean. I've been there."

I shook my head. It was the worst day of my life. "Where's Mickey?" I asked, changing the subject. I was as tough as old Elmer. No whining for me. No way. "Where'd he go?"

"Poor young fellow got a little spooked," Elmer said, resting his head against the wall. The old man was hurting, there was no doubt about it. He twisted his lips around his teeth and blew air out his nose.

"So where'd he go?" I asked again.

"Well, I'll tell ya. Me and him talked a while about Normandy and the war and this here tornado. The boy is a walking encyclopedia when it comes to tornadoes. Anyway, we just shot the breeze for a while, waiting for help to come. But the wait got to him. He got to fidgeting around, looking out the window every couple of minutes."

My legs felt like lead weights, so I sat down beside the old man.

"Then he sees this truck go by. Weaving through all the junk in the street. Mickey thought it might be you coming back with the reinforcements. I told him you knew where the place was. But he said, naw, he was sure it was you. So he hightailed it out of here, fast as he could go, to flag down the truck. I ain't seen him since."

"How long ago was that?"

Elmer fumbled in his pants pocket and pulled out this old-fashioned watch on a little chain. He flipped open the top and looked at it. "Seventeen minutes ago," he said. "Time ain't exactly flying around here."

"Listen," I said. "There's help on the way. A state trooper is sending some National Guard guys in a Jeep to get you to the hospital. They should be here any minute."

"Ah, I'm all right. I reckon there's lots of folks worse off than me."

A tough old bird.

I stole a glance at the doorway. No Mickey. Where in the world had he gone?

"Why don't you go look for your friend?" Elmer said. "He couldn't have gone far. But I reckon it's pretty spooky out there. You go and have a look-see."

"I don't want to leave you."

"I ain't going nowhere. You go find Mickey. Even I'm getting worried, and I ain't no worrier. Go on now."

I wasn't sure what to do. I mean, where could Mickey have gone? I kept thinking about the poor dead guy and the dog with his guts blown out. Elmer was right. It was spooky out there. No telling what could happen. *Oh, geez, Mickey, where are you?*

"Go on now," Elmer said. "That's an order. I'm the senior officer here. You go find your friend. He's a good boy. He might need you. I'm fine."

I stood up. My legs still felt heavy. "Well, okay. Just for a minute. I'll go find him, and we'll be right back. We won't leave you. I promise."

"Go!" Elmer snapped.

I went. Across the wreckage of Java River, out the door, over the tree in the hallway, through the depot. Out into the dim yellowish daylight. Out into the post-tornado landscape. Where in the world was Mickey?

I ran out in the middle of the street. There were no cars or anything. In fact, there was nothing moving. There was no one around. Just the train signal clanging in the distance. I spun around and around. Looking, listening, hoping. Where could Mickey have gone?

Sometimes you don't have to see anything to know something's going on. Sometimes you can just feel it happening somewhere out there. Like a hunch.

My hunch told me to take off north of the End of the Line. Move straight down Castle Street. See what was down there. See if Mickey had gone in the same direction, chasing after the truck Elmer had mentioned.

So I jogged down the middle of the street, dodging the cars and tree limbs and junk that littered the street. Not real fast. Just a good, steady pace.

My hunch paid off. Big-time.

Two blocks down Castle Street I spotted Mickey. He was standing on the sidewalk, facing away from me. His hands were planted on his hips, which were swallowed up in Uncle Pat's sweatshirt with the stupid joke on the front. He was just standing and staring.

I started to call to him, but I stopped when I saw what he was watching. Suddenly all this awful-tasting goo rebounded out of my stomach into my mouth.

At the end of the block, just a few feet from where Mickey was standing, three guys were hauling stuff out of a house. The house looked like it had been bombed—gaping holes in the plaster, glass and bricks and wood debris scattered all over the neat little lawn. The front door had been blown off its hinges, and these guys were hauling stuff out of the opening as fast as they could—a TV, a VCR, a computer. They tossed their loot in the back of a mud-caked blue pickup truck and raced back into the half-destroyed house for more.

Looters. That's what the state cop had called them.

Rednecks. That's what Mickey had called them. The people from Raven Glen. I recognized the lead guy. Red Man. The goon that had run Uncle John out of the Circle K. He and his buddies were looting the houses that had been trashed by the tornado.

The idiot rednecks were having a ball. Red Man had his cap tilted back at a jaunty angle and was laughing at something one of his friends said. He had his thick arms wrapped around a big television set, happily wobbling toward the truck. His mouth was joyously working on a wad of tobacco.

The other two rednecks looked like escapees from the Texas Detention Center for the Criminally Insane. They were both hard-looking men, mean and scary. Their eyes were wide windows of hate and anger. They were probably in their mid-thirties, their faces covered with beard stubble, their legs encased in grimy jeans. One of them was blond, with his stringy hair tied back in a ponytail. He had a scraggly Fu Manchu moustache. He was carrying a microwave.

The third guy looked like he had swallowed a bowling ball. Skinny legs carrying this distended stomach. He had on a crusty white T-shirt. He must have been some kind of farmer—his face was burned leathery by the sun. He was missing most of his front teeth. He wore a stained green John Deere cap. He looked like a composite of all the wanted posters I had ever seen at the Dallas post office.

After Red Man deposited his TV on the tailgate of the pickup, he pulled a pint bottle out of his back pocket, took a long drink, and handed the bottle to Fu. Fu just about drained the contents. Farmer took a more modest swig, and Fu playfully punched him on the arm. All three of them roared with laughter. They made looting look like a lot of fun.

Apparently the rednecks didn't see Mickey.

How could they miss him? He was standing on the sidewalk just a few feet away from the house. Looting must take lots of concentration.

I started to call to Mickey, but nixed the idea because it would only call attention to him. I opted to wait until the rednecks went back into the house, then charge down the street and pull stupid Mickey behind some shrubs or something. Then the two of us could race back to the End of the Line and wait for the National Guard to come and help Elmer. We could tell the soldiers about the looters.

Good plan. Didn't work.

Fu spotted Mickey just as the three looters started back into the house. He pointed at Mickey and yelled something. I was too far away to hear.

Run, Mickey, you doofus. Run!

The clanging of the signal bell in the distance seemed to get louder.

Red Man took another swig from the whiskey bottle, wiped his mouth on the sleeve of his blue jean jacket, and started walking toward Mickey.

I dropped down behind the trunk of a mammoth oak tree that had blown across the middle of the street. There was a thick branch sticking straight up, and I got on my knees and peered between the trunk and the branch. All of me was covered except one eye. The rednecks would never see me. Not that they were looking.

Everything smelled wet and sour. The signal bell kept clanging.

Red Man approached Mickey like he was a wild horse that might bolt and run if he wasn't careful. The redneck stopped a few feet from where Mickey was standing and said something.

Mickey just stood there like an idiot. Hands on his hips. Just standing there like his stupid feet were glued to the sidewalk. I knew Mickey. I knew what was wrong. Mickey was too scared to move.

I couldn't hear what Red Man and Mickey were saying. I was too far away and the dumb train signal drowned them out. But I could read their lips a little and fill in the gaps from their hand gestures.

What are you lookin' at?

Nothing.

Don't look like nothing to me.

No. Honest. Nothing.

You look familiar. Don't I know you from somewhere?

No. No way.

You ain't gonna tell nobody what we're doin', are you?

No. Nobody. I'm just looking for help. There's this old man back at—

You gonna tell the cops, ain't you?

No. I was just looking for somebody to help me with this old man. . . .

I stayed on my knees. My heart was pounding so loud I

thought the rednecks might hear it. The sound was so piercing I thought I might drown out the train signal. My armpits suddenly reeked.

Red Man shoved Mickey in the chest with the palm of his hand.

Run, you blockhead.

Mickey stumbled backward and rubbed his chest.

Red Man shoved him again.

Okay, Kenny. Let's go! Time to move!

Only I didn't move. I just kept watching, safe behind the tree trunk.

Let's go! What are you waiting for? Mickey needs help. Now!

Fu and Farmer trotted over to the sidewalk, where they formed a circle around poor Mickey. My roommate looked confused. And scared.

Now, Kenny! Move! My legs hugged the ground. For some reason all I could think about was the dead guy I had found earlier. How awful his body looked. I couldn't get the image out of my mind. And the dog. With his guts all over everywhere. My brain was suffering image overload. One-armed man and dog spun and twirled around and around. I was dreaming while I was still awake.

I blinked and shook my head. Red Man slugged Mickey in the face.

Now! Now, Kenny! Move!

Fu kicked Mickey in the leg.

I couldn't breathe. I couldn't move. I knew what I needed to do, but nothing happened. My legs vanished. Sour stuff poured out of my stomach into my mouth. I was so scared, I was bawling. I couldn't help it. The sky was this awful red-orange color. The train signal clanged louder and louder. The whole earth stank from Mother Nature's fart.

Suddenly I realized I was banging my forehead against the tree trunk. Slowly at first. And then faster and faster. Harder and harder. I didn't even feel it. Not really.

Red Man slugged Mickey in the stomach, dropping him to the ground.

Tough Kenny, 'fraid of nothing. 'Fraid of nobody. Yeah, sure. There he was—big, brave Kenny Francis—crouching behind the tree. Hiding. 'Fraid of everything. 'Fraid of everybody.

Fu kicked Mickey in the head. Then the three rednecks walked away.

For some reason, the clanging train signal suddenly stopped.

CHAPTER 18

I FELT AWFUL. Who wouldn't? I had camped on my duff and watched a bunch of stupid rednecks beat up on my best friend. While I just sat there. That and bang my head against a tree trunk. Lotta good that did.

It didn't matter that things turned out okay. That was irrelevant. I mean, it was great that the National Guard guys came by in their Jeep about two seconds after the rednecks left Mickey on the sidewalk. The Guardsmen chased Red Man and his buddies away, loaded Mickey in the Jeep, picked up old Elmer at the End of the Line, and took both of them to Bedford General.

Everything turned out fine. The doctors fixed Elmer's leg and put in two stitches under Mickey's eye. And gave him two aspirin. Mickey didn't have any broken bones or anything, just cuts and bruises. He stayed at the hospital less than an hour. He was okay.

Except I felt awful.

After the Guardsmen drove off I hiked back to the gym, and nobody knew I had even been behind the tree. Nobody knew I had watched what the looters did to Mickey. Except me.

Over the next few days, I thought about what had happened. I replayed the scene again and again in my mind like some videotape you watch over and over, waiting for something to change. Only it's always the same.

Kenny stumbles over a mangled dog and finds the dead body of a guy who looks like his math teacher. Then Kenny loses his cool completely, watches his friend get knocked around, turns chicken, and sneaks back to the gym with his tail between his legs. The same movie every time.

Should I tell Mickey? That was a tough question. Mickey was all pumped up about the whole thing. He told me the story—over and over. The stupid doofus was thrilled to death about it all. He had never been in a real fight in his life. Now he had taken on a gang of redneck looters single-handedly and had the scar under his eye to prove it. And he wasn't hurt. It made a great story.

So I swallowed my tongue and let him tell his tale—again and again. And then Mickey went home to San Antonio.

There wasn't any reason to stay. The day after the twister hit, Mr. Wellington closed the school until after the first of the year. Smart move. Bedford Academy was a mess. No water, no electricity. All the windows blown out. So Mickey headed home.

And I never said a word.

But the whole thing kept eating at me. Gnawing at me like some kind of disease. It wasn't the end of the world or anything, but it didn't feel good. I mean, I was not proud of myself. And I really didn't know what to do about it.

Not that I wasn't busy. I spent the week after the tornado in overdrive. My mom was in Houston getting people to think positively, so I stayed with Uncle Pat in Bedford.

We worked our tails off. Every morning we got up before dawn, ate breakfast real fast, and spent the day helping the tornado victims all over town. I mean, we did everything. The Red Cross people gave me an armband, and I served soup and coffee one day, sifted through tornado rubble one day, stacked lumber and stuff one day.

But I still felt awful.

Uncle Pat felt awful, too. Only for different reasons. He was bummed all week, seeing his little town destroyed, his school closed, his life topsy-turvy. The whole thing really got to him. Every morning he went out and tried to help friends and neighbors whose homes had been damaged or leveled. Then he spent every evening with his buddy Jim Beam. He'd curl up in his blue corduroy chair and stay up all night reading history books.

A couple of times at the dinner table I started to tell Uncle Pat what had happened that day. But I lost my nerve. What would he think of me? It wouldn't be good, I'll tell you that.

So I just kept it inside until the weird stuff went down.

The weird stuff started late Saturday night. I mean real late, like about three in the morning. I rolled over in bed and heard this sound. But I couldn't tell what it was. So I got out of bed and tiptoed out into the upstairs hallway. It was dark and cold. The sound came from Uncle Pat, downstairs in his La-Z-Boy. He was singing. Not real loud, and not real good. But real soulful. The way drunks sing. With lots of feeling.

I sat down at the top of the stairs, wrapped my arms around my knees, and listened. Uncle Pat was singing an old song called "Wake the Town and Tell the People." Only he wasn't singing the right words. He had rewritten the song.

> Strafe the town and kill the people,
> Drop your napalm in the square,
> Take off early Sunday morning,
> Get them while they're all at prayer.

It was freezing in the hallway. Winter cold settling in the old house. I hugged my knees real tight.

> Drop some candy to the orphans,
> Watch them as they gather round,
> Use your twenty mill-i-meter,
> Mow the little Commies down.

I leaned my head against the banister. I was stuck in the house of sadness. The world of night. Listening to the song, I felt really close to Uncle Pat. It was a song about horrible things happening in Vietnam, about people doing horrible things.

> Strafe the town and kill the people,
> Waiting for their pound of rice,
> Hungry, skinny, starving people,
> Isn't killing Commies nice?

No wonder I went back to bed and slept until one o'clock the next afternoon. Nights are tough in the house of sadness.

The next day I threw on a black Guns 'n Roses T-shirt and the same pair of jeans I'd been wearing for the last week and came downstairs. I made myself a peanut butter sandwich and opened a bag of Fritos.

Uncle Pat was still in his bedroom. He was taking Sunday off. So was I. We both needed a day of rest.

I was still a little foggy, not paying much attention to anything, just munching my peanut butter and Fritos and staring out the kitchen window at the gray day outside.

"I've about had enough of this. How 'bout you?"

I looked up.

Uncle Pat stood in the kitchen doorway. He looked shaky. Too much booze. Too many late-night history books. Too much tornado. Dark circles framed his eyes. His skin was the color of buttermilk. Stubble dotted his chin. He had on a red flannel hunting shirt that could have subbed as a tarp in Texas Stadium. The shirt hung down over a pair of jeans that constituted half the world's denim supply.

"What's going on, Kenny?"

"When life gives you lemons, you should make—"

"Please don't say it." Uncle Pat grabbed a carton of orange juice out of the refrigerator and sat down across from me at the kitchen table.

I finished my sandwich.

"To be honest with you," Uncle Pat said, "I feel like the tornado swept you up and took you to Mars. You're not really here anymore."

Maybe I wasn't as good an actor as I thought.

Uncle Pat drank the orange juice right out of the carton. "All week you've just been going through the motions," he said, wiping his mouth on the back on his hand. "Granted, you've done a great job of helping people in Bedford, and for that I'll be eternally grateful. But when we talk, it's . . . well, strange. You keep asking about Bobby Kinkaid, and I've told you again and again—your dad and I played on the same team with him, and he was a good player who blew out his knee. End of story. But you keep asking. Then if you're not asking about Kinkaid, you don't say a word. I know the tornado has something to do with it. I mean, it's traumatized everybody. But Kenny, give me a break."

I picked up sandwich crumbs off my plate and sucked them off my fingertips. Uncle Pat took another swing of OJ. Then we sat and listened to the ticking of the grandfather clock in the hallway.

Then I told.

I couldn't help it. It was driving me nuts. I told Uncle Pat about hiding behind the tree in the street and watching the redneck looters whip up on Mickey. I told how I lost my nerve and didn't do squat to help my friend. I told the whole thing.

Uncle Pat just sat and listened and nodded like he understood. He was good at that. He chewed on his lower lip a little, but that was it.

Believe me, it was not easy to tell. And, to be honest, I didn't feel any better after I told. Everybody says that if you've got something bottled up inside, you'll immediately feel great if you just tell somebody, let it all out. Not really. You just feel like you dropped your pants in public.

But it was okay. I didn't cry or whimper or sniff a lot. My voice didn't break. I just told how Kenny turned to Jell-O when his best friend needed him. It was a simple story.

When I finished, Uncle Pat filled his cheeks until they swelled and then blew all the air out with a rush. "I appreciate your honesty," he said. "I know that was hard for you."

I nodded. That was a start.

But then Uncle Pat left. He just got up and left the kitchen table without another word and vanished into the hallway. Is that weird or what?

I didn't move. I didn't know what to do or what to think. I'd told Uncle Pat the deepest, darkest secret of my whole life, and he just got up and walked out of the room.

Thanks a lot. I mean, I'm sure he was ashamed of me. I was ashamed of me. But to just walk out?

After a while I heard Uncle Pat's voice on the phone upstairs. I couldn't hear what he was saying, just this low murmur. Surely he wasn't phoning Mickey in San Antonio? Not without talking to me. Uncle Pat wouldn't do that.

I stared out the window at the gray day. I didn't know what else to do. Then Uncle Pat came back downstairs. I was really surprised. He was all dressed up—blue dress shirt, gray slacks, blue blazer. Shaved face, combed hair. He leaned against the doorjamb in the kitchen.

"Okay," Uncle Pat said. "You were honest with me about something that's been bothering you. Now I need to do the same. So I want to give you an early Christmas present."

"Is this really the time for a new bike?" I couldn't keep the sarcasm out of my voice.

"It's not that kind of a present. Kenny, you're old enough to know that the best presents, the ones that matter, can't be wrapped up in shiny paper and opened on Christmas morning. The best presents are always something else. This is something we should have given you a long time ago. I've set it all up. It's something that has to be done. Especially now, after what you just told me. Go change. We need to leave in fifteen minutes."

Uncle Pat is a good-natured old fat guy, but I always have the feeling that underneath he's like a volcano or something. There was something in his voice that let me know it was time to get my rear in gear. So I did.

But I didn't get it. What was going on? Where were we going? Who had he called? What was this Christmas-present stuff he was talking about? I was major confused. So I went upstairs and put on a maroon shirt and a clean pair of jeans. And this really cool black and yellow ski jacket Uncle John gave me for my birthday. And an Atlanta Braves baseball hat. Backward.

Fifteen minutes later we were in the Accord, backing out of Uncle Pat's driveway. "So where are we going?" I asked politely. I hate mysteries. I hate surprises. I hate not knowing what's going on.

"You'll know when we get there." Uncle Pat seemed really pleased with himself. Like he was taking care of some long-overdue business. He swung the car into the street, put it in drive, gripped the wheel with both hands like they teach you in driver's ed, and we were off. He wasn't going to tell me where we were going. Not even a hint.

Uncle Pat concentrated on his driving. I suspected that was so he wouldn't have to look at Bedford. He wouldn't have to see all the wreckage from the tornado. There was nobody out. It was too cold and damp and gray. It was too depressing.

I slumped down in the seat and stuffed my hands in the pockets of my ski jacket. Whatever was gonna happen, I was just along for the ride. Uncle Pat cleared Cherry, drove past the Circle K where I'd first seen Red Man, and headed up the ramp to the interstate. Wherever we were going, it wasn't in Bedford. I trusted Uncle Pat, I really did. No matter how weird things got. A boy needs a father.

CHAPTER 19

SNOW STARTED FALLING ABOUT THE TIME WE HIT DALLAS.

It was a real Texas snow, wet and slushy, blowing all over the place. Sticking in patches on the side of the road, making the streets glisten. Making you feel damp even if you were inside a car just looking out the window.

Technically it was still daylight, but all the cars on the Central Expressway had on their headlights. Everybody drove slowly.

Uncle Pat hunched forward, concentrating on his driving. He didn't want to talk. Neither did I. The windshield wipers pounded out their steady rhythm. *Boom, swish. Boom, swish.* The car heater was up too high, making the inside of the Accord smell like an old furnace.

By the time we pulled into the parking lot of Cajun John's, the snow had started to stick to Big D. The parking lot was icy slick, and the Accord skidded a little as we pulled into a space next to the building.

Since it was Sunday, Cajun John's was closed and the parking lot was deserted. Except for Uncle John's cherry-red 300ZX, which was covered with snow and starting to look like a big candy cane, and Uncle Larry's white Taurus, which was fading into the snow. The rest of the lot was a white field, silent and cold and damp.

Uncle Pat and I got out of the car and made our way to the front door of the restaurant, our shoes squishing in the snow. I plunged my hands deep into the pockets of my ski jacket. My breath hung in the air in thick wisps, like I was smoking. I looked up at Uncle Pat, hoping for an explanation, a word, some reassurance. Anything.

I got nothing. Uncle Pat just nodded at me to open the door and go on in. He followed me through the door, then closed it behind us and locked the deadbolt. Strange things indeed.

The restaurant was dark except for a single bank of lights over Uncle John's booth in the back. I had to squint to see that far, but I could see Uncle John and Uncle Larry seated at the booth.

"Go on back. They're waiting for us." Uncle Pat's voice was a whisper.

I shrugged and started for the back of the restaurant. As I walked past the entrance to the bar, I could see the snow falling through the mammoth window. The white stuff was covering the parking lot and the street beyond, making the whole world look clean and white. It was cold in Cajun John's. It was also shabby. I mean, without a million people eating and drinking and dancing and rocking and having a big time, the place was a little threadbare. For the first time I noticed the carpet in the lobby was worn in the center and frayed on the edges. The bayou paintings were faded where the sunlight hit them. The fishnets on the walls were full of holes. The smell of stale beer and cigarettes clung to the air. Everything was dusty. Little dirtballs gathered in packs in the corners of the room.

I slid into the booth beside Uncle Larry. Uncle Pat slid in beside Uncle John, facing us. For this weird minute the four of us just sat there in the empty, dark restaurant and stared at each other.

Somewhere inside of me I knew whatever was about to happen would change everything forever.

"You want a Coke? Maybe some coffee?" Uncle John asked.

I shook my head.

"Coffee. Black." Uncle Pat's face was pale. He needed more than caffeine.

Uncle John nodded and turned over a white mug on the table. Then he filled the mug with coffee from a high-tech thermal bottle. He gave Uncle Larry a coffee refill.

My three fathers looked at their coffee. I looked at them. No doubt about it. Something big was about to go down.

Uncle Pat cleared his throat. "This is my meeting," he said. "But it's a meeting that should have taken place a long, long time ago." He paused to stir his coffee, which was weird because he was drinking it black.

"Kenny, Pat says you're really low these days," Uncle Larry said. "You're hurting, and it's hurting us."

This was gonna be worse than I'd imagined.

"Kenny, we've talked about this on the phone," Uncle John said, "and the time is now. A lot of what's going on is our fault. Mine and Pat's and Larry's. We . . . ain't done right by you, kid. We need to get some stuff off our chests."

Uncle Pat cleared his throat again. He leaned back and looked at my other fathers. "Fellows, here's the story in a nutshell. Kenny told me about something that happened the day of the tornado. You don't need to know the details, but trust me when I tell you it was a courage thing. Not a macho deal. A courage thing. Okay?"

Uncle Larry and Uncle John nodded their agreement. They exchanged a quick glance, and I had the feeling Uncle Pat had just told them a lot. Like a secret code had just passed between them.

For my part, I felt relieved. Nobody else had to know what had happened that day. It was just between me and Uncle Pat.

"It's time you knew something, Kenny," Uncle Larry said.

"Way past time." Uncle John drained his coffee cup.

"It's time we get the courage thing straight," Uncle Larry said in his best preacher voice.

"What are you talking about?" My voice came out in a high-pitched squeak. The whole thing was making me nervous.

"We're talking about your real dad," Uncle Pat said. "We're talking about Dickie."

"Huh?" I looked away from my fathers, past the empty booths, through the bar, out the big window at the snow falling on the parking lot. It was getting dark. The snowflakes were coming down hard. No more drifting. Now the snow was being hurled from the heavens.

"Over the years," Uncle Larry said, "we've done you a disservice, and to tell you the truth, I think we've done Dickie a disservice."

"What are you talking about? What's going on here? Why are you guys acting so goofy?" I couldn't seem to control my mouth.

"Larry's right, man," Uncle John said. "Just listen. Please. That's all you gotta do. That, and know that we love you."

Now I really was nervous. Uncle John never says stuff like that. Never, ever. He might take you to the Super Bowl or slip you a little Jack Daniel's in a Coke, or palm you a twenty, but he never says stuff like he loves you.

"Let me start," Uncle Pat said, finishing his coffee. "Let me tell you about your dad and Vietnam. He—"

"I already know about all that. How he saved the platoon and was this big hero and how everybody liked him and how—"

"Be quiet, Kenny. You don't know anything." Uncle John rested his head on the padded back of the booth and closed his eyes.

"Kenny, to be honest," Uncle Pat started again, "we

haven't been entirely truthful with you. Sometimes, over the years, we've exaggerated some of the stuff your real dad did. Not much. But some."

I looked Uncle Pat right in the eyes. I inhaled through my nose. When I exhaled, it came out "Bobby Kinkaid."

Uncle Pat nodded. "Yeah. Bobby Kinkaid. The truth is, Bobby Kinkaid was a super high-school football player. Your dad played on the team."

"So what about all the stories about the great games my dad played?"

Uncle Pat winced. "They were Bobby Kinkaid stories. I just substituted your dad in the story. In truth, Dickie was the other halfback. Mostly he blocked for Bobby. At the time I was telling you the stories, I didn't think it mattered."

"But the stadium. Francis Field . . ."

"Your dad died in the war. He was a Bedford grad. I was on the faculty. I pushed a lot. It didn't have anything to do with how good a player Dickie was. Kenny, your dad was a good player. But not the star, like I told you."

I leaned back in the booth. "I kinda suspected this was coming," I said. "I saw this newspaper clipping at Mom's. I guess I figured it out. That and the story about the basketball player from New York City. Mom said my dad was a terrible basketball player. He didn't really smoke the city dude, did he? That's just a story, isn't it?"

My three dads checked out their empty coffee cups. "Yeah, right," Uncle John mumbled. "The New York guy smoked your dad real bad. Dickie shot his mouth off, bet a bunch of money, and the city dude aced him, fifteen to nothing. And it wasn't that close.''

"Okay, so you guys wanted me to be proud of my real dad. That was nice. It's no big deal. I'd already pretty much figured it out. No harm. I forgive you. Okay?''

Everything got real quiet.

"There's more,'' Uncle Larry said.

I swallowed hard. I wasn't sure I wanted more.

"It's about 'Nam,'' Uncle Pat said. "Seems like the story of our whole generation is about 'Nam. Anyway, Kenny, there's one thing you gotta understand. Vietnam was hard on Dickie, I mean, really hard. It was hard on all of us, that's for sure. It was the worst thing in the world. We'll never get over it. But it was unbelievably hard on your dad.''

For the first time in my life, I had absolutely nothing to say. I slouched down in the booth and jammed my hands into the pockets of my ski jacket.

"It wasn't just the heat and the mosquitoes,'' Uncle Pat went on. "That got to everybody. And it wasn't the rot and the trots. Everybody had to deal with that.''

Uncle Larry and Uncle John nodded. They weren't smiling.

"And it wasn't even the lack of sleep,'' Uncle Larry said. "Or even the fear that at any given time you might die or get mangled or see a buddy go down. I mean, any given time. On watch. On patrol. Every night when you'd lie down to sleep, an incoming rocket might get you. Charlie might slip up on you and slit your throat. Death was in the air all the time. It wasn't any of that. Or maybe it was all of it.''

"Dickie was in over his head,'' Uncle Pat said. "I knew him better than anyone. We had played ball together at Bedford and at SMU. Roomed together for four years. He and I were closer than brothers. So I knew what the war was doing to him. He cried every night. Bawled his eyes out. He was so scared.''

"I don't want to hear this.'' And I didn't.

"You got no choice,'' Uncle John said.

"I think you'll understand in a minute,'' Uncle Pat said. "First you need to know about the big mistake we all made.'' He stopped and looked at the ceiling. When he looked back at me, his eyes were damp. "The three of us kidded Dickie about being so scared. It was just a macho soldier thing to do. We were just young guys. I guess we thought if we teased him about being such a chicken, he'd snap out of it.''

"Only it didn't work,'' Uncle John said.

"Sure it did,'' I shot back. "My dad saved the whole platoon. He—''

My three dads stared at me. They just stared. As if they wanted to tell me something without saying the words.

"Kenny.'' Uncle Pat groped for the words. "There's no good way to tell you this. But the fact is . . . your dad didn't save the platoon, like we told you. The fact is . . . Dickie killed himself. He just couldn't take it anymore. He couldn't take Vietnam and the fear and the teasing. He couldn't face us. So one morning about dawn, he just walked away from camp and ate his gun. That's what really happened. A few minutes after it happened, the VC staged a raid. A couple of other guys got shot. A couple of other guys died. It happened every day. We just listed Dickie as a casualty in the raid. It was easy.''

"We shouldn't have teased him," Uncle Larry said. "We shouldn't have made fun of him. It was our fault. Dickie was losing it bad. We should have realized what was happening to him. Gotten him some help. But . . . we just didn't.''

Suddenly nobody was looking at me. All three of my dads were looking at the snow in the distance, looking into their coffee cups, checking out the ceiling.

"So this has been our big family lie," Uncle John added. "And it ain't done any of us any good."

"We've let you down, Kenny," Uncle Pat said, "by creating the myth of Dickie's perfection. I don't even remember how it started. Somehow it just happened. When we started telling about him, the stories just got better and better. It was like we could make it up to him by making him a hero. We didn't plan it or anything. It just happened."

"But it was stupid," Uncle Larry said. "It was stupid because we didn't love Dickie because he was perfect. We loved Dickie because he was Dickie."

"He was human," Uncle Pat said. "Nothing more. Nothing less."

My real father wasn't a big football star who saved his platoon in Vietnam. My real father got scared and killed himself. Plain and simple.

I felt like I had been kicked in the stomach. My mind

was racing. I felt dizzy. What I really felt was crazy. Everything I thought I knew was wrong. I wanted to sprint out of Cajun John's. Except my legs wouldn't move. They weren't connected to my body anymore. Nothing seemed connected anymore. It was like a free fall through space.

"We created the myth," Uncle Pat said, "with the inadvertent help of your mother and your grandmother. We made Dickie a hero. Bigger'n life. But the fact is, Kenny, your dad was very human. I loved him, but believe me, he was human. Like all of us, he made mistakes."

"Like?"

"Okay. I'll tell you. The honest, no-holds-barred truth, Kenny, is your dad was having trouble at school. About to get kicked off the football team at SMU. He had a wife and a baby on the way. He had too many responsibilities. That's why he joined the marines. It didn't have anything to do with patriotism. Dickie was just looking for a place to hide."

Free fall through space. *Everything I know is wrong, wrong, wrong.*

"We've all made our share of mistakes," Uncle Larry said. "All of us. Like lying about Dickie. He doesn't deserve it, and neither do you. We've given you a legacy nobody could live up to. The legacy of a perfect father. It's a crock, Kenny, and believe me, we're sorry. You'll never know how sorry."

"We've forced you to try to live up to a lie," Uncle Pat said. "Kenny, listen to me. Courage is not like we told you. It's not charging machine gun nests. It's not whipping everybody's butt. It's not winning at everything.

Courage is facing life. It's admitting mistakes. Courage is trying to be the best person you can be. Courage is hanging in there. Courage is being true to who you are. To what you believe in. It's what you did in the aftermath of the tornado. That's what courage is. It doesn't have anything to do with never being scared. Everybody gets scared. I mean, everybody. You, me, Dickie. Your dad was a good guy, but he wasn't perfect. And we should have told you that a long time ago.''

Uncle Larry and Uncle John nodded. Then silence fell over Cajun John's like the snow that was covering the ground outside.

My dads suddenly looked old. And tired. And relieved. Like three guys who'd just figured out how great it felt when they stopped hitting their thumbs with a hammer.

And me? I leaned back in the booth and closed my eyes and let it all sink in. *Everything I know is wrong.* I'd been living in a world of lies. All my life my real dad had been the greatest football player, the top student, the star, the BMOC, the big war hero. Guess again.

My real dad was an average guy who got scared and blew his brains out. I couldn't think of anything to say. I guess there wasn't anything. I wasn't really mad. Actually, I felt relieved to know the truth. To be let in on the secret. I knew my dads really loved me. So we all just sat there in the empty, dark restaurant and watched the snow fall outside. And thought about Dickie.

CHAPTER 20

CHRISTMAS IS USUALLY THE PITS.

But not this year. This year it's cool. I mean, the whole thing is still pretty tacky—pressure to buy Christmas gifts, endless reruns of the stupid Jimmy Stewart movie on TV, silly Santas trying to sell you stuff, everybody trying to be so happy when they're really not. But this year none of that bothered me much. I just rose above it all.

I even had a good time at my mom's annual Christmas party. Not the easiest thing in the world to do—Mom gets tense and nervous and nothing ever turns out like she wants, and a lotta people don't show, which hurts her feelings. Stuff like that. Don't ask me why she has the thing every year. I usually hate the party, but this year it was a hoot.

Mom hadn't cleared the boxes and junk out of the hall-way and living room of her new condo. But that didn't stop her; she had her party anyway. People from work, old friends from SMU, my three dads. It seemed like everybody she'd ever met was there. And you know what? It was fun. She and I put up a tree and hung ornaments on it. And put out some stupid Christmas decorations that were about a hundred years old. We put old-time Christmas music on the stereo, served champagne and stuff from the bakery. Everybody was joking around and laughing and having a good time. Even me.

I snuck champagne in a paper cup with Santas all over it and hung around in the corner of the condo just watching people and thinking about stuff. That sounds cheesy, but I had fun.

Everything seemed really clear to me that night. Like all the stuff my dads laid on me in Cajun John's. The big family lie. My guess is that most families have one. Somewhere. It may not be as dramatic as ours, but I bet they have one.

I mean, I felt sorry for my real dad. Killing himself and everything. But in a lotta ways it was nice to be out from under the shadow of Super Dickie. My dad had just been an average guy. Believe it or not, that felt a lot better than having a dad who was so great at everything.

I did feel sad about the way he died. And I felt sad about how my other dads made up all that stuff. But the thought occurred to me the night of my mom's Christmas party that I had a choice in this. I could feel sad about it as long as I wanted. So how long should I pout about it? A week? A month? A year? Till my twenty-first birthday? Forever? Not much point in that.

It happened a long time ago in a place I'll probably never even see. To a father I never even met. I wish I had known my real dad and I wish he hadn't done what he did. But he did, and right now I feel pretty lucky. I survived the worst tornado in the history of Texas. I've found some good friends at school. My mom and my other dads love me a bunch. And I can't change any of what happened in Vietnam or after, so why not let it all go? Sounds good to me.

How about staying mad at my dads and punishing them for what they did? I don't think so. If you think about it, they've been punishing themselves for years. Take Uncle Pat. Hiding out in his house all alone, with just history books and wine. So he won't have to think about it.

And Uncle Larry. If he can win enough souls for Jesus, then maybe God will forgive him for what he did in the jungle a lifetime ago. And Uncle John. Life's a giant toy store. But are there enough toys in the galaxy to make him forget? I doubt it.

So why should I add to their punishment? My dads are doing a good job of that themselves. And I do love them. Which is the main thing.

I even thought for a while about getting mad at my mom and G.G. After all, they went along with the big family lie. Even though they didn't have a clue what really happened in Vietnam, they made my dad sound heroic and everything. They loved my dad and wanted to believe he was a hero. Mom and G.G. added their own wrinkles, exaggerated the good things, left out any bad stuff. In their own way, everybody wanted to make it up to my dad, so they made him more heroic than he was.

So I considered getting sore at Mom and G.G., but what's the point? They miss my dad every day. Why punish them? It's time for all of us to put the lie behind us and get on with life.

I think the main reason I enjoyed Christmas so much is that I'm excited about the future. Yeah, me. Excited about the future. How about that?

After the first of the year I'm heading back to Bedford. I'm gonna graduate next year. I'm finally gonna finish something. I'm going out for the soccer team this spring. I won't be the star, but that's okay. I really do like to play. And I'm gonna haul my guitar back and practice some. That's something else I enjoy.

Most of all, I'm looking forward to rooming with Mickey. I miss his encyclopedia and his off-the-wall facts. He's kind of a dork, but I really like him.

Am I gonna tell him about what happened the day of the tornado? Probably. Good friends shouldn't keep secrets like that. Having a lot of secrets just messes you up. Do I think Mickey will understand and forgive me? I don't doubt it for a minute. Mickey's a good guy.

While I was sitting there in the corner of the condo, sipping my champagne, I remembered the camping trip I took with Uncle Larry years ago. The one where I went out in the middle of the night to pee and couldn't find the tent in the dark. That night I couldn't see anything, I mean nothing, so I stumbled around, waving my hand all over the place, groping the air, feeling really lost and really stupid. And then, all of a sudden, my hand brushed the tent, and I was safe. Just like that.

That's how I felt the night of the Christmas party. Like I had just found the tent.

ABOUT THE AUTHOR

JIM LESTER was born in Little Rock, Arkansas. He graduated from Southern Methodist University and went on to receive a master's degree from Vanderbilt University and a Ph.D. in history from Washington State University. A former college professor, he has written several books on regional history. He and his wife, Camie, live in Colorado, where he teaches history and English at Denver Academy, plays racquetball, and writes fiction.